AF225648

STRANGER

EDITED BY
Paula Dias García,
Sam Agar,
Marc Clohessy &
Aran Kelly

LIMERICK, 2024

Sans.
PRESS

STRANGER

ISBN: 978 1 7391383 7 0
Published by Sans. PRESS
July 2024
Limerick, Republic of Ireland

COVER ARTWORK & ILLUSTRATIONS by James Fenner
LAYOUT & BOOK DESIGN by Paula Dias Garcia
TYPESET in Bookmania and Ferryman

EDITORS
Paula Dias Garcia, Sam Agar,
Marc Clohessy & Aran Kelly

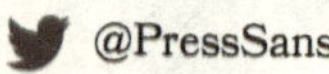
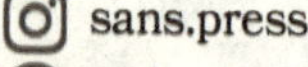

www.sanspress.com
@PressSans
sans.press
/sans.press

STRANGER receives
financial assistance from the Arts Council.

Paula Dias Garcia

Editor's Note

We were asked, at one point, to describe Sans. PRESS in terms of what we'd be in a forest. After cycling through a number of very tempting lies – gorgeous flowers, long-living trees, exciting animals – we ended up landing in the only thing that rang remotely true. *A handful of mushrooms,* we said. *You know, the kind you find when you lift up a rock?*

Because, if we've strived for anything so far, it is to be the weird ones in the clearing. If we've been doing it right, we hope to be keeping you – our readers – on your toes, no matter if this is the first of our collections to reach you or (can you *believe* it?) the seventh.

And, very true to name, *Stranger* is our weirdest one to date. I'd be doing ourselves, you, and our writers a disservice if I tried to fit all of these stories under one label, one neat bow that ties the whole thing together, so I won't. I'll tell you only to think of a bunch of mushrooms you found under a rock. They might make a delicious meal, or they might be unthinkably poisonous; they might be ancient or brand new; beautiful or downright disturbing; they might thrive under darkness or be steadily fighting to reach the light. The only think you can really know by looking is that you can't look away – they're fascinating, they smell delicious, and they're calling for you.

And what echoes behind all of the stories in *Stranger* is the persistent challenge of trying to know others – and the reminder that it might be equally impossible to fully know ourselves.

In this latest collection, there are doubles that reflect the worse in us, and doubles that smooth hard edges; transformations brought on by true belief or by scheming plans; and unexpected bonds that come from the shadows, from inside or from beyond! Once again, the hardest part of putting *Stranger* together was having to pick from all the mind-bending (in the best way!) works we got to read.

As ever, we are so grateful to every writer that trusted us with the work, the lecturers and booksellers supporting our project, the Arts Council and every single one of our readers!

Welcome to the woods – follow the trails, look under rocks and forage for mushrooms! Just, you know, mind the poison.

The Stories

Content Warnings

Harvest of Shadows: injury detail, large scale death

The Starving Feeling: drug misuse, mental distress

Rent: body horror, violent death

Haire: injury detail (of an animal), serious illness (referenced)

Them: body horror, large scale death

The Treachery of the Heart: injury detail

We Came Travelling: sexual abuse (implied)

Satellite Office: war (referenced), blood, injury detail

"As Gregor Samsa awoke one morning
from uneasy dreams he found
himself transformed in his bed
into an enormous insect."

The Metamorphosis, **FRANZ KAFKA**

"They did not speak, they did not bow,
they were not acquainted; they saw each other;
and, like the stars in the sky separated by millions
of leagues, they lived by gazing upon each other."

Les Misérables, **VICTOR HUGO**

Lauren Mulvihill

Myself and I Alone

I first met my sister the morning of Daddy's burial. She was lying in a ditch near the chapel, her skin all scraped by thorns, little wounds spitting crimson driplets of blood on the foliage around her. I wondered if she had risen through the earth to find me. We looked a lot alike.

Aren't you only after going and falling into the ditch, I said to her.

Not fallen, she said, just unable to stand. And I've a funeral to attend.

I held my hand out to her and she wrapped her wet fingers around my wrist. The ditch was sodden with the runaway water of a nearby river. A thorn cut shallowly into her right cheek as I raised her, leaving a long interrupted trail like a sewn hem on her face – her face, which was also my face. She adjusted the strap of the old, mud-caked leather satchel she had thrown over one shoulder, the kind Daddy used to carry his woodworking tools in.

Is it your father who's dead, I asked her.

'Tis, she said.

Dead this Monday past? I asked.

Being buried today in the church just behind us, she said.

In which case, I told her, your father is my father, and the two of us are sisters.

We walked hand in hand to the chapel where Daddy's old stone body lay in its burnt-sugar box, handmade by the man himself. We were late to the party, so the priest was reciting his sermon already, and I wanted to tell him it was no use, 'cause if Hell was real then our Daddy was already burning there.

The only place he's going is into the soil, said my new sister.

The two of us laughed sharply. The priest lost his place.

By this time, some of her blood had wet the cuff of my white blouse and I felt at once that we were close, as close as two people could ever be, and I didn't know her name but I felt that she could not be a stranger but truly my sister, a woman whose face I shared, my half-sister: a term which suited us fine since we were two halves of a whole, one babe torn apart by King Solomon. When the Mass was over Daddy went out on the shoulders of the funeral director and her three sons, and when he was lowered into his lowly plot my sister and I both bent our backs and spat on the head of his coffin.

After the burial we went into town, and only once we were sat in Delia's cafe did we let go of each other's hands. She was covered in dirt and she smelled of it too. I told her I'd pay this time, no worries at all. I ordered a fruit scone with butter and cream and blackcurrant jam made in-house, and a cup of tea with no milk and no sugar, and she asked for the very same. I shook my head in disbelief while we ate at how I, who this morning had no one, had now myself and everyone. Our mothers, we discovered, had even given us the same name, "Geraldine", through sheer coincidence and lack of input from our father.

I can't believe, I said, I can't *believe* he never told me about you. I can't *believe* I've gone my whole life not knowing I had you. And we're so alike, you and me, aren't we? Looking at you now, I said, it's like looking in a mirror.

A mirror, indeed. Our noses bent sideways in different directions. I wanted to ask her how she'd broken hers.

It's amazing he spoke to you at all, she told me then, and my heart broke for her. Which is better, a body and soul all lost at sea or a ghost in the house, a heart buried in the garden? I suspected this was not the first day Ger had mourned her father. She said he just planted her one day, and was gone.

And your mother, I asked, is she living or dead? Was it from her you found out about the burial?

Dead, said Ger.

And mine, said I. God, we're so alike, aren't we?

She moved in with me that evening, into the boiling attic bedroom above my own, above the fruit and veg shop our father had owned. She hadn't much to bring with her, only the clothes on her back and her leather satchel, and the clothes were now mud-stained and ragged. No matter, I told her – we were both the same size. I gave her the pick of my clothes. I dragged the heavy chest of drawers from my bedroom out into the hall while she bathed, and I left it at the foot of the attic ladder, so the two of us could more easily share.

It feels like home, she said when she climbed into her room for the first time, wearing my spare set of pyjamas.

Where have you been living until now, I asked her.

D'you know something, she replied, I can't remember.

I said it's a pity himself had to die in the middle of July, because the attic was hot, hot, hot; too hot in the summer by half, hence why I'd since taken his room, meaning she'd be in my childhood bedroom. Ger wasn't to worry at all, though, because the shop downstairs was a cold concrete slab of a place, and air-conditioned as well, so we'd be nice and cool at work the next morning.

Can I really come and work in the shop? She asked from the top rung of the ladder, her torso twisting like a wizened tree trunk to look back at me.

Of course you can, of course you can, I said. It's *our* shop, Ger, left to Daddy's kin.

I'll take your bag, I said then, because she was clearly laden down by the weight of it, and the strap looked close to snapping. She told me in harsh and certain terms that I wasn't to touch her bag ever. Ever. Sisters are like that, I hear: dramatic. I wished her sweet dreams and got ready for bed. I fell asleep that night with a smile on my lips, thanking God and all who'd listen that my father was dead.

When I snuck out early the next morning with grand designs for breakfast (Ger would have what I'd have), I was surprised to find her already up and dressed and standing in front of the chest of drawers, running her knuckles across the varnished dark wood. She wore a long sleeveless sundress, beige in colour like the bare walls and contents of the house itself. Her skin was all clear of scrapes and bruises. She looked part of the furniture already.

Tell me about this, she said, still absently stroking.

The chest of drawers? Daddy made them. They're legacy pieces, I suppose, made to outlast him. He even grew the trees himself. He was green-thumbed.

Hence the greengrocer's, she said. Her palm paused to hover over a swirling pattern of curls and vines he'd drawn in pale, inlaid wood.

Yes, I said, and on that note, you'd want to change your clothes, my love, into something more sensible. That dress will get destroyed downstairs. Breakfast?

I can hear him in it.

Breakfast, Ger?

She did change eventually, into jeans and a rough-hewn tartan shirt she must have found in the bottom drawer, and after she came downstairs with that full-to-bursting satchel hung around her neck we took breakfast together in the garden. I baked warm fruit scones and made crunchy bowls of muesli, all served with tart yoghurt and glistening red jam and thick clotted cream, with freshly-squeezed orange juice to drink in tall glasses.

Your father made these, my half-sister said, of the wooden table and chairs we were sitting on. She drank her muesli from the bowl, both hands cupped around it.

I must admit I was rankled by this, because I'd hand-made the scones and the juice and the jam and so forth and she'd made no such remark about them. I told her I'd sooner burn the chairs and the table, but times were hard and furniture cost money.

They're made from the same tree as the chest of drawers, Ger told me.

I'd sooner get rid of them, I repeated, and I took a very deliberate sup of orange juice.

Oh no, Geraldine, not these ones. They're his legacy, remember.

She ran the pads of her fingers across the surface of the table.

Ger stayed back to wash the dishes while I went down to open the shop. I'd closed the place for Daddy's funeral, and just one day of closure had left it feeling haunted. The bare concrete walls of the back room were cold and dry despite the heat outside, and when daylight sept through the open doorway and into the windowless darkness my eyes played a trick on me. I saw the unfamiliar shape of my father where, the lightbulb soon confirmed, there were only cobwebs and stiff waxed coats on hangers. I gathered some empty plastic crates and left the room quickly.

My half-sister was, like me, a good worker, and after we had the shop set up I spent some moments just looking at her lovingly, and she back at me. Eventually she had to flip the door sign on my behalf from "closed" to "open", or I might never have done it.

I'll never be lonely again, I said, and then Fintan Prendergast was in the door with his empty bottles for refilling.

Fintan was an absolute fossil of a man with a penchant for my home-squeezed juices. He stopped quite abruptly in front of Ger and looked her up and down.

'Who's that?' he asked me then, pointing at her.

'My half-sister Geraldine,' I replied. 'We call her Ger.'

'She's like your father,' said Fintan, his ancient jaw bobbing up and down, chewing on himself.

'I also look like my father,' I said.

'Yeah,' he said, 'but she *is like your father.*'

And he left with nothing. I told Ger that a gentle breeze would bend Fintan Prendergast out of shape, so she wasn't to take his attitude to heart. She said it didn't bother her. Later I caught her standing in front of the mirror on the wall beside the counter, eyes searching our face for the traces of a dead man. She was still looking at herself when it came to dinner that night, at the distorted reflection in her silver soup spoon, which was entirely stealing her attention away from the carrot and sweet potato soup I'd prepared.

We look terribly alike, don't we, Geraldine? she said to me. She sounded miles away.

We look the same, I told her. It's amazing. I've never felt so close to a person.

Yes, she said, and she slipped the clean spoon into her satchel, preferring instead to lap up the soup with her tongue, like a dog. I'm glad to have found you, she said.

I saw our father's ghost today, I found myself telling her, feeling foolish but knowing I shouldn't hide such things from her, from myself. I saw him in the corner of the back room downstairs.

He's in the soil, she said.

Soup dripped down her chin.

The following day, Ger woke early to make our breakfast. The salty smell of frying meat permeated the house, and I found our chest of drawers wide open and rifled through. My clothes were strewn about inside. I pushed each drawer tightly closed to prevent any grease getting into the fabrics. My hands lingered for a moment at the top, searching for whatever special quality hers kept finding in the wood. I felt nothing more special than the taut rigor mortis of a dead tree. It never seemed fair that so cold a man could make something so beautiful, when beauty should surely be warm. I looked back through the open doorway of my new room, his old room, dark and a bit hazy through the frying pan's smoke. I looked up into the open attic above my head and I thought of the rafters there, damp and creaking in the summer heat.

That night I climbed the ladder and slipped into the bed beside my sister, the two of us smelling of earth. She slept like a corpse, flat on her back. I dreamt of roots, and woke up with dirt on my eyes.

Time travelled slowly with Ger at my side, always in my clothes, always with that bag on her hip. At night we slept parallel and perfectly mirrored. Our voices and manner of moving became so alike that I sometimes forgot we were separate people at all. I had to look hard at the bend of her crooked nose, which leaned a different way to mine, to remind myself that we were on opposite sides of a mirror. We stopped speaking once we knew we could read each other's thoughts. I smiled at her often, to show her she wasn't like Daddy, as Fintan Prendergast said – she wasn't cold and distant like frozen deep soil; she was a sun-baked river at summer's end, warm and fresh and lively. As time wore on she took over the cooking. She caught meat in the fields nearby, and I never told her not to; I welcomed the break, welcomed being minded. I brought her vibrant fresh vegetables from my garden. She peeled off the skins with her sharp nails. At night we slept like mirrors, slick with sweat in the hot attic room, a heavy leather satchel in between us.

When Fintan returned to the shop in early August, finally lured by the siren song of crisp apple juice, Ger was in the back room and I at the till. Their first interaction had left her wary of customers, so we typically were only ever apart when a person came through the shop door. In that sense, I suppose, she was a bit like Daddy, though his was a selfish reclusiveness which left me more often lonely than alone. I'd learned the family business that way: through neglect. I had to, or we'd have had no money. He never sold his carpentry.

Fintan came in, anyway, heavy head swinging around on his thin neck, eyes wide and cautious. He held four empty milk bottles in hand, ready for refilling. I retched and coughed up a wet thing, like a clump of earth, onto the counter, and quickly wiped it away.

'I was wondering if you'd ever be back, Fintan,' I joked. My voice was a bit strained. 'I'm drowned in juice.'

'Is she around?' he asked me, whispering, still hovering at the threshold.

'She's in the back there,' I said.

He hurriedly filled his four bottles to the brim with the fruit juice I kept on tap by the door. Scuttling across the room, he hauled them onto the counter and took his time rooting around in his pockets for money.

'This building is cold,' he remarked. A single bead of sweat crept down his long nose.

'It's nice in this heat, isn't it?' I said.

'That woman is like your father,' he warned.

I gave him more change than he was owed and started separating the bottles into two canvas carrier bags. With a very serious look on his wrinkled face he dragged one bottle towards himself and unscrewed the lid. Holding it steady with both his shaking hands, he brought it to his lips and took long, deep gulps of the sweet liquid until he was gasping for air.

'You're an artisan,' he told me breathlessly.

'Thank you, Fintan,' I said, smiling. I screwed the cap back into place and packed the bottle away before pushing the bags towards him.

He looked long and hard at the dark smear of dirt on the side of my hand.

'She'll bury you, that one,' he said, and left.

He moved slowly out the door with his heavy bags, too proud to ask for help, too stubborn to accept it if offered.

When the bell rang to announce his departure, Ger came out of the back room with two great sacks of spuds thrown across her shoulders and three more in her arms. The satchel bounced gently against her hip as she walked. She moved weightlessly. All ten of her fingernails were black with dirt.

She set the bags down near the window and tore open the largest of them. When she bent her back to dig through it, sunlight caught the contours of her strong neck and arms, squeezed into an old t-shirt of mine that fit her perfectly not long ago. I covertly squeezed the thickest part of my bicep between my fingers, and what I felt there was soft and loose on the bone, looser than I remembered it being back when I knew myself by touch and reflection, and not just by the face of my sister. I stood in front of the roughly-cut mirror on the wall and examined the grey skin of my shrunken cheeks.

Through the mirror I watched Ger pick a dirt-caked potato from the heavy white sack, a great round stone-like thing, and sink her teeth deep into its raw flesh with an almighty crack. She turned to me and smiled, her mouth a gaping hole. I let her know I was feeling unwell and I hurried upstairs to vomit black bile on the floor of Daddy's bedroom.

At dinner I sat in silence on one of the first chairs my father made, both me and it unsteady. I studied Ger's movements while she stood over the stove with her back to me. I watched her scrape the skin from vegetables with her nails, blood forming under them where a sharp bit stuck, blood dripping into the boiling pot of water when she didn't wash it off her skin. I watched her tear some anonymous animal to bits with her hands. I saw the hard muscle in her body where I had only thin skin and soft fat and creaking bone, and I saw the unreserved speed with which she moved from here to there, like she knew the place better than I ever could, like she didn't need to hesitate or tiptoe or close doors quietly or move in a way that was any bit apologetic at all. And the bag, the bag, the bag still hung around her neck.

I got up and pulled down on the strap. My sister whirled and slapped me hard across the face.

That night we slept apart for the first time, she in our father's room, I in the muted beige sweatbox of the too-hot attic. What little sleep I stole was plagued by visions of roots and the dirt that encased them, growing everywhere, seeping into all there was. The sound of shattering glass announced the morning, as Ger took a hammer to every mirror in my house. I brushed black soil from the sunken hollows of my eyes and cheeks, and the sharp points of tiny stones tore at my skin. Climbing down from the attic, I found Ger standing over the chest of drawers, lovingly stroking the surface with hammer still in hand.

Who was this stranger I'd taken into my home? Who was this person who was so like me and so unlike me? With the mirrors gone she was my only reflection, and I was sure we were rapidly growing in opposing directions: she was stronger, more beautiful, more forceful by the day and I was shrinking, I felt it, in body and soul. She cooked for me, cleaned for me, spoke at the till for me now, for she'd learned – or had taken – that skill from me too, and I was in the attic, in the rafters, in the hot, hot dark alone again, lonely and quiet and bored, thinking of Fintan and what he'd do when his fruit juice ran out. She locked the doors the day she broke the mirrors. I couldn't leave, and each morning I woke with dirt on my eyelids, dirt bursting out of my mouth. I reeked of decay.

I saw her now at meal times and that was it. The kitchen these days was dim and reclaimed by nature, all covered in wet dirt and fungi, so we always ate in the garden, which was her preference anyway. She was radiant in the sun, but the heat made me weak. My bones always creaked like the rafters upstairs. Some days I could hardly see through the wet clods of dirt packed over my eyes.

One evening, when the summer was nearing its end and the wind was cooling, she sat me down at Daddy's table and served me a bowl of soup. Lumps of earth and stone floated around in it. She picked them out of hers with her fingers. I could hear her strong jaw crunch down hard on the rocks. Her whole body, even that ever-present satchel, shuddered with the effort of it. In front of us, in the small stretch of grass that made up her back garden, the sapling of something reached up from a long and unsettled mound of tilled soil, stealing the light from my slowly-dying vegetable patches.

What's that, Ger? I asked.

It was the first time we'd spoken in weeks. I no longer understood her face, so I couldn't read her thoughts anymore. If ever I could.

It's a tree, my love, she replied. We're green-thumbed.

She smiled at me. Her chattering teeth were blood-stained. The strap of that bag dug chokingly into her throat. I wondered if a soup spoon could cut through old leather.

She went to work the next morning, locking the front and back doors and all the windows behind her, while I searched for knives. I told her I was looking for mouse droppings but I needn't have lied because the knives were all gone, all of them. Ger always cooked with her fingers and hands; she got rid of the knives a long time ago. Any axe or good tool was in the shop downstairs. Choking on the globules of earth that came up through my throat like phlegm, I snatched two silver spoons from the sink and lurched into the hallway. I opened wide the chest of drawers our father had made. I picked out the beige dress she'd worn that first day and I held it to my breast, burying my nose in the fabric, seeking some fresh scent that wasn't death, damp, decay. Pale spots of mould dappled the hem.

I took the dress in my fists and ripped it apart seam-by-seam, and when they were all ripped I tore into the fabric itself, reducing it to rags. I reached into the drawer for the next garment, and the next, and the next until I was red in the face and choking on the stones inside me. I'd sewn these seams myself in many cases, some seams of shirts that once were his. I dropped each pitiful rag on the floor and laid hands on the heavy wooden chest that was built to outlive me. With the tail end of my soup spoons I carved into the varnished wood, carved deep and clear lines, gouging and splitting the surface with terrible shapes that sullied the cool, careful craftsmanship with red-hot ugliness.

When I finished I sank to the ground, spent, and sat there with my head against the chest's frigid surface until I had the breath and the strength to get up and close the attic ladder. I went into Daddy's bedroom to sit, to wait. On the floor beside Ger's bed, a mound of dirt and stone covered the dry pool of my vomit. I craned my neck to look through the small latticed window above the bedframe. Outside on the road, old Fintan Prendergast was shuffling quietly away from my shop, four empty bottles in his hands.

The door closed heavily when she returned around four o'clock, the skinned carcass of some creature dangling from her fist. She dropped it with a thud when she saw what I'd done. I watched her through her bedroom door, watched her stand at the chest of drawers and start to weep. She ran her fingers erratically over the criss-crossed slits I had carved. She looked more like me then than she had in some time. Throwing her arms out wide, she fell upon that thing they so loved, hardly aware of me behind her, even when the wooden bedframe groaned as I pushed myself to standing. Ger didn't startle when I placed one open palm on the back of her head and pushed our face into the furniture.

I took hold of the strap of her old leather satchel in my empty fist and pulled down roughly on it. It snapped in two easily, like a worn length of twine. The heavy bag crumpled onto the pile of my torn-apart clothes and fell open, spilling dark, viscous soil like blood across the carpet, and beneath my hand I felt hair turn to moss and skin and bones to silt until the stranger was no more. I plucked a silver spoon from the dirt and held it up to the light, where my eyes played a trick on me. I saw the distorted shape of my sister's face in the spoon's convex reflection, when really it was mine. I looked like I'd been dragged backwards through a ditch.

I got out my hoover and sucked up the soil. I emptied half of it into a canvas carrier bag, lay the dead creature on the carpet inside, and tipped the rest of the stony dirt in on top. I pulled my keys from the rotting front pocket of that old leather satchel and went out to the table in the garden, where I took a heavy wooden chair and brought it down firmly on the dried corpse of the sapling in the grass, crushing it to dust.

With the canvas bag thrown over my shoulder, I left my father's house and went, huffing and puffing and red in the face, out past Delia's cafe and onwards to the graveyard he was buried in. The ground hadn't settled yet on top of him. I tipped the soil and the creature out onto it and packed it all down with the sole of my boot. I was covered in dry dirt; it clung stubbornly to my hands, my hair, my eyelashes and clothes. As I stepped away, I caught my haggard reflection again in the gold plaque on his wooden grave marker.

I went to the river that ran behind the graveyard and followed its course to a wide and shallow stream. It had been baking all day in the overhead sun, kept safe on all sides by ancient trees and quietening birdsong. There, in the sidling dusk of autumn, I took off my bag and my clothes and I lay down in the shimmering water. My mud-caked body, hot and chafing with stale sweat, gradually cooled as the river ran over and past me, until soon I felt chilly-warm and clean. Long weeds like horse's hair and thick green flowering plants tickled my arms and legs and painted my purpling skin with goosebumps. I wondered if I had risen through the earth to find this.

LL Garland

Harvest of Shadows

It's easy to dismiss Nightgaunt.

Among a small but vocal online community, it's universally believed the Austin band created one of the worst albums in the history of thrash metal with their 1994 release, *Here Lies Nightgaunt*. With songs such as the aural assault "Walkin' on my Grave" and the painful power ballad "Her Mts. of Madness" the quartet cemented their status as one of the greatest disasters committed to vinyl. Perhaps most excruciating was their closer, "Damaged, Ink." – Nightgaunt's torturous answer to the question Metallica never asked them.

Despite their lack of commercial success, the band has found lasting infamy due to the mystery surrounding their final show. My ongoing personal fascination with Nightgaunt's demise has become a running joke at the Dis/Chord Magazine offices. However, when legendary Editor-in-Chief, Sunny Jackson, learned of the existence of security footage of Nightgaunt's last show, he knew this was my chance to uncover the truth behind the tragic sudden deaths of one of heavy metal's worst bands and a bar full of their fans.

For years, Nightgaunt reliably booked gigs in the thriving Austin music scene based on their ability to draw a crowd of two to three dozen people. Usually, just supportive family members and a few addled fans, which was good enough for the clubs to allow them onstage. Keep in mind, this was the early days before Austin was AUSTIN.

The band consisted of four friends from the city's garage scene. Singer, rhythm guitarist and songwriter, Fred "Fretty" Lance saw himself as one of the great voices of hard rock, rivalling Ronnie James Dio himself. In reality, his voice often cracked and his stage growl was known to draw laughter from the audience. But Fretty's stubborn delusions were the glue holding the band together, providing opportunities they took full advantage of.

Fretty was joined by childhood friend Domingo Reyes on lead guitar. Dom's clinical dependence on the distortion pedal fooled him into believing technical skill was irrelevant to success. Dom was known – and feared – for his ability to wedge a guitar solo into any moment.

The lone bright spot in the band was bassist Sam Garber. Like a female Lemmy, Sam would sneak bass power chords into songs, lending their performances at least a passing resemblance to metal. It is a sad reflection on the masculine subculture of metal in that era that a woman of her talent was relegated to laying down the pulse for Fretty's lifeless lyrics. However, her burgeoning songwriting skills were on full display on "Pyrrhic Victory," easily the most listenable song on their album. Fretty only agreed to include it after Sam convinced her father to finance the recording of *Here Lies Nightgaunt.*

Dom's cousin Guillermo Reyes rounded out the band on drums. Memo seemed to suffer acute bouts of tendonitis as he would often take mid-song breaks from pounding the skins to rest his sticks. Unknown to his bandmates, on the night of their last gig, Memo was weeks away from earning his EMT certification and likely quitting the band.

Their names would have fallen into obscurity if not for the suspicious and unexplained circumstances surrounding that final show.

Contemporary police and news reports are vague. All we know for certain about that night is that Nightgaunt played a set and no one left The Red-Eyed Boar alive. Investigations concluded that it was carbon monoxide poisoning caused by a gas leak, but the advent of the internet and early chat rooms kept the metal mystery alive through decades of rabid speculation and conspiracy theories.

And that's where it would have ended – a few obsessed old metalheads, sharing theories ad nauseam on the internet. But a few months ago, a member emerged on a Nightgaunt conspiracy chat room, using the handle **@MetalUpYourAUS**, claiming to be the son of The Red-Eyed Boar's former owner. He insisted he was in possession of the security footage showing everything that happened that night. **@MetalUpYourAUS** backed up his claim, posting a grainy ten-second video time-stamped to October

16, 1996, the night of the show. When questioned by the community – *Why wait until now? Why didn't you give this to the cops? Why won't you just tell us what happened?* – **@MetalUpYourAUS** listed the footage on an auction site, saying only 'see for yourselves.' A bidding war ensued among collectors and committed conspiracy theorists with Rae Ancira placing the winning bid.

You may remember Rae Ancira as the lead singer/guitarist of the all-girl speed band, The Koffin Belles, in the 1980s. Rae had developed a friendly relationship with Dis/Chord's editor, Sunny Jackson, after he profiled The Belles in '84. When Sunny heard Rae had the key to unlock the enigma I'd been chasing my entire career, he contacted her, asking if Dis/Chord could screen the footage. Rae kindly agreed. That's how I wound up in a leafy hillside neighbourhood of West Austin, wandering the living room of certified platinum rock royalty and her menagerie of rescue animals, excited to uncover the conclusion of one of rock's greatest unsolved mysteries.

Rae greeted me at the door wearing Joan Jett eyeliner and combat boots, flanked by two large pit bulls. Her hair has gone prematurely silver but is cut in the same choppy style from her days in The Belles. After a warm welcome, Rae invited me in and gave me a tour of her vast memorabilia collection accompanied by the clingy dogs, Eddie and Murray. Rae is an avid metal historian and collector of rock arcana, and her stash did not disappoint. The pride of her collection is a case of tiny bones resting on black velvet, said to be from Ozzy's bat – sans skull, of course.

Rae guided me to her living room, where a slim brown paper package awaited us. The return address on the label read only "The Red-Eyed Boar, Austin, TX." The envelope was still sealed. When Rae noticed me staring at it, she shrugged and said, 'I've been too excited slash nervous to watch it alone. I just hope I didn't blow twelve thousand bucks on this and it turns out to be some dude's dick pics.'

I sat on the couch with fifty-five pounds of Eddie curled up in my lap and asked Rae if she knew anything more about the shadowy **@MetalUpYourAUS**. She had never spoken with him directly but didn't believe he was really related to the club owner. All of her communications had been exclusively with the auction company, which closely guards their clients' privacy.

'Seems kinda shady,' she admitted. 'Probably just a manager or bartender who stole the tape before they shut the place down.'

Rae ripped into the envelope and loaded the disc. The giant screen filled with the familiar images of a half-packed, seedy club. The footage was divided into four different angles: the stage, the bar, the audience, and the door. The video was queued up to the point when the band took the stage.

Rae sat beside me on the sofa and asked, her voice shaking with anticipation, 'Are you ready to finally find out what happened to Nightgaunt?' With a nod from me and a snore from Eddie, she pressed play.

The footage proceeded exactly as I'd expected. Fans have circulated bootlegs for years, claiming to be from the final show. The more reliable ones I've listened to all perfectly matched what we witnessed, including the banter between songs.

Instead of the show ending where I expected, however, the band remained on stage. With a sneer at his audience, Fretty announced, 'I wrote this next song last night. It's the darkest death metal you ever heard. S'called "Ceaseless Slaughter." Get your affairs in order, assholes. Shit's about to get dark.'

With one or two groans and a flurry of devil horns from the audience, Fretty counted in the band. It was what you'd expect from an unpracticed disaster. Fretty screamed into the mic and pounded his guitar. Dom played a few supporting riffs, then launched into an unrelated solo. Sam tried her best to pull everything together while Memo struggled to find the beat once or twice before deciding to sit the song out.

If those bootlegs truly were from this night like they appeared to be, they didn't include this new song or anything after. Which begs the question: why? Why cut the song? Why omit the one moment of the night everyone wants to hear?

At this point in the footage, one of the patrons at the bar got up and left.

'That was Lester,' Rae said, pausing the tape.

Lester Burnett had been a regular at The Red-Eyed Boar and the last person to leave the club alive that night. He gave a statement to police then disappeared from history, cementing his status as primary suspect among Nightgaunt's fans.

These next few moments of footage would confirm or refute once and for all what the online Nightgaunt community had been obsessing over for decades. Arguing the exact wording of the police reports. Postulating that the coroner must have been paid off. Blaming everything from aliens to demons. Some believed Lester was a mass murderer. Others thought it was a Robert Johnson deal with the devil situation gone wrong. People found links to a 1923 creekside tent revival outside Shivers, Mississippi where believers sang for three days straight before dropping dead. Or the more recent death of a cellist in a locked practice studio in Tokyo. Trolls joked that Nightgaunt had killed their fans by playing the worst song in history (which, judging from the intro to "Ceaseless Slaughter," was a distinct possibility). One persistent poster declared on numerous occasions that an 'angel of mercy had swept down from heaven and taken their souls for the sin of metal music. Repent before it's too late.' The only thing everyone could agree on was that you couldn't believe the police reports.

Regardless, once Lester left, whatever transpired inside The Red-Eyed Boar went unwitnessed by a living soul until the bouncers came in for their share of the tips at the end of the night and found four dozen bodies littering the floor. Both bouncers swore in their affidavits that no one had been in or out except Lester once the band went onstage. For his part, when asked why he left early, Lester told the police, 'I've had to listen to those shitheads mangle their old songs every Monday for months. Fifty-cent Lone Stars ain't gonna get me to suffer through them practising their new garbage.'

I nodded at Rae, ready to finally see what really happened. 'I'm gonna keep it muted from here on out, y'know, at least our first time watching… just to be careful.' Rae flashed a sheepish grin. My heart fluttering, I thought of all the wild theories about a song with the power to kill a club full of fans and gratefully agreed. Rae hit play.

Everything seemed normal. Fretty was working up a good head of steam, growling into the mic with abandon. I only noticed one laugh from the audience, most were good-naturedly thrashing each other in front of the stage while those at the bar minded their drinks.

That's when he arrived.

A man stepped out of the shadows, conjured between one moment and the next, clutching a guitar case. His entrance hadn't been picked up on the door camera and he hadn't emerged from the office. He was simply there when one moment before he hadn't been. The thin, hunched man in a rumpled suit, wearing the sort of hat only hipsters or my great-, great-grandfathers once wore, strode towards the stage. The camera that had been facing the office followed him, tracking the man's weaving path through the audience, then zooming when he reached the stage. He took out a battered old twelve-string and sat on the edge of the stage, facing the audience. The case was propped open at his feet like a busker playing for loose change.

It took a while for anyone to notice the man perched on the stage, just where the light met shadow. Dom Reyes was the first. Unsure how to handle the invasion, he motioned to Fretty for direction. Reading Dom's lips, he clearly asked Fretty, 'What the hell, man?'

Without missing a beat, Fretty stalked across the stage, stared down at the man and planted a boot in his back.

Despite the force of Fretty's kick, the man didn't move, didn't even acknowledge Fretty's presence, only carried on tuning his guitar. Fretty tried to dislodge him again, this time reaching for the neck of the man's instrument.

Before Fretty could grasp the old guitar, the man started strumming. The security camera zoomed in close enough to make out the chords. His fingers flew along the fretboard at a pace that would've put Dimebag Darrel to shame. Several things happened in that moment: **1.** Fretty froze, then backed away from the man, a peaceful expression replacing his outrage. **2.** The faces of the audience turned as one towards the interloper. **3.** Rae and I gasped, both realising the man had seven long, pale fingers on each hand.

He strummed left-handed, in a complicated style somewhere between mariachi and blues. His right hand glided along the neck like warm honey, fingers dancing between frets in a complicated waltz.

Rae was leaning forward, elbows on knees, covering her mouth with black-nailed fingers. For my part, I was seeking comfort and reassurance from the warm, soft body of Eddie the pit bull, my hands stroking his silky fur. It was uniquely unsettling to see a roomful of people begin singing and swaying, ignoring the band on stage, rapt in a song I could not hear.

Even that I could've explained away, but once my eyes landed on Fretty's shadow, I felt the malevolent nature of the man's song. The singer's shadow was no longer content to hide behind Fretty from the stage lights, a squat puddle of darkness aimed at the rear wall like those of his bandmates. Instead, it stretched forwards into the light, reaching towards the busker's case. It grew longer and thinner until the shadow hands touched the case, clutching the rim like a life raft. A mass of many-handed shadows joined it from the direction of the audience. Although Fretty – and the audience – swayed in time with the man's music, his shadow did not.

In the grip of the busker's song, Fretty joined his guitar with the man's, strumming chords he'd shown no previous capacity for.

That's when I noticed the humming. Rae, her eyes creased with strain, stared at the man's hands flowing across the fretboard. She was humming, working out the melody as he strummed, hesitant at first. Then she grew more insistent and began to vocalise the notes, swaying in the grip of the music just like Fretty and the audience. Hearing only a few bars of the mournful song in her raspy, contralto voice sent shivers through me. It felt like long-buried miseries stirring, being laid bare by the intricate melody.

I shoved her once, twice, then snapped my fingers between her eyes and the screen. Only Murray's distressed whimpers as he bumped his head into her ribs broke the music's spell. Disappointed anger flashed across Rae's face before she came to her senses, like someone waking from a dream. When I told her what she'd been doing, her face turned ashen. She apologised and closed her eyes for a moment, hands clasped in her lap to keep them from shaking.

By the time our attention returned to the screen, the drinkers and employees had joined the audience. Their shadows darkened the floor, pooling around the guitar case.

Memo was also lost to the busker's song, pounding a steady rhythm on his drums. Only Dom and Sam remained free of the man's tune. Dom was reaching across the drum kit, slapping his cousin. Sam tried to keep playing "Ceaseless Slaughter" on her bass while pulling Dom away. When she got his attention, it looked like she mouthed, '–intro to "Pyrrhic Victory."'

Dom nodded and launched into the devastating opening riff. Sam joined, stance defiant, feet spread wide, thrashing her low-slung bass. Soon, however, Dom's attention began to fail. His eyes darted away from his fretting hand to Memo and Fretty, wild-eyed terror etched on his face. Sam planted herself in front of Dom, locked eyes and challenged him to a call and response. Trading riffs, the bandmates united in a desperate guitar battle against the relentless pull of the busker's tune.

But for once, Dom couldn't be relied on to lose himself in a solo and remain distracted from what was happening around him. Each time Dom glanced away, Sam jabbed him with the head of her bass. Never one for practice, Dom's hands grew leaden. His strumming weak, placement sloppy. When he took a break to stretch the cramps from his fingers, the song took him.

The busker threw back his head in a triumphant howl. Only he didn't actually howl. His thralls threw back their heads and did it for him. Every mouth in the club gaped wide, gleefully victorious. All except for Sam and the stranger. The man lacked a mouth. His face, formerly hidden under his hat, was a flat expanse of taut pale skin, his only features slippery black eyes that shone like obsidian.

Sam played on, resisting alone for as long as she could. Ricocheting between the riffs in every metalhead's arsenal without a beat's rest. She bounced from "Holy Diver" to "Breadfan" to "Ace of Spades" and many I couldn't identify from the muted video.

Meanwhile, her bandmates circled around her, playing the busker's song while a few audience members climbed on the stage to join them. They formed a swaying, slowly tightening circle around Sam. She clamped her eyes shut and focused on her music. Hair clung to her face in sweaty clumps. Blood poured from cracks in her fingertips. Nails ripped away from flesh. Still, she kept pounding the blood-slicked strings, beating back the creeping shadows.

Despite the television being muted, I would swear I could hear the moment when the bone between the second and third knuckle of her pointer finger snapped. Even then, Sam kept playing, dragging the finger along the strings, the snarl on her face the only evidence of her pain.

Then her second and third fingers snapped. She was left with only her pinky to fend off the darkness. To fend off surrender.

But that was too much to hope for. We already know how the story of Nightgaunt ends.

The snarl fled Sam's lips, replaced by a blank complaisance. Her stance relaxed and she slowed her pace to strum a walking blues bass line. Every living soul in The Red-Eyed Boar was singing and swaying to the busker's tune while Sam's shadow extended to join her bandmates' at the guitar case.

The pale creature strummed his final chord with a flourish. When his pale hand reached its zenith, everyone in the club crumpled lifeless to the ground like marionettes whose strings had been severed.

Now free of the bodies that once tethered them, the feet of their shadows slithered across the floor and hopped inside the case.

The busker knelt and placed his guitar within, nestled in the shadows. Then he cupped his hands and scooped up a wriggling stray shadow, guiding it into the case like a baby bird fallen from its nest before shutting the lid and snapping the latches. Stealing past the bodies of the fallen and favouring his left side, where he carried the case, the busker picked his way across the club like an overladen ship listing in rough seas. He disappeared in a blink.

Rae and I sat in stunned silence, watching the unnatural stillness of a rock club gone quiet. The only sound in the room was the pounding of my heartbeat in my ears. I stared at the heap that was Sam's corpse on the stage, willing it to move, to twitch. But I knew she wouldn't.

Then the screen went blank. Rae stood beside the DVD player, disc in hand. She cracked it in half, then cracked each piece in half again. My stomach lurched with each snap. Part of me in protest, now we'll never hear the song with the power to slay dozens of people at once.

Rae rushed outside, the ever-present dogs on her heels. Too troubled to remain alone with the memory of what I'd seen, I followed and found Ray hovering over an old bar-beque grill, emptying a can of lighter fluid over the flames before tossing it and unloading another.

We sat together as the sun went down, watching the coals as they burned to grey ashes. Long after dark, after hours of silent vigil, I stood to leave. I only made it a few steps across the lawn before I had to turn back and ask Rae the question that had been gnawing at me all evening.

'Do you think we destroyed the only copy?'

I imagined somebody finding an unaltered, undestroyed bootleg somewhere. Maybe a disc lurking in someone's garage or a cassette stuck inside an old Walkman at a thrift shop.

Rae's unmoving silhouette was silent for a long time. Perhaps she didn't hear me or didn't want to think about it. I started to cross the yard again, making my way to my car, when I heard her say in almost a whisper, 'God, I hope not.'

On my drive back to the hotel, I decided to swing by the music district downtown. After a few wrong turns, I found my way to the corner of 8th Street and an unnamed alley where The Red-Eyed Boar once stood.

The old building was long gone. What was once a dingy club on a dirty little side street had been knocked down to make way for a well-lit upscale high-rise condo building.

I was disappointed to find that the ground-floor corner where The Red-Eyed Boar once stood is now home to a high-end steakhouse frequented by legislators from the nearby capital and the lobbyist who curry their favour with wagyu beef tartare and expensive whiskey. I doubted any of them had lived in Austin long enough to remember The Red-Eyed Boar. They certainly didn't look like the type to have heard of Nightgaunt.

I stood on that corner, struggling to believe that the otherworldly massacre I'd witnessed just hours before had taken place in such a banal location. Occasionally, the doors swung wide, pouring bloated men in rumpled suits and women with strained cheeks and gaudy jewels into the streets. Soft piano music chased them out and joined the ever-present Austin soundtrack of electric guitars and traffic.

At times, I thought I could hear echoes of the busker's song in the noise. But I convinced myself it was just jetlag combined with the unbelievable footage making me hear things, making me jumpy.

Near midnight, the music was interrupted by the rattling wheel of a homeless man pushing an overflowing grocery cart up 8th Street. As he got closer, I realised he was humming a tune. Perhaps it was just my overstretched mind or the fact that I hadn't eaten since breakfast, but that tune raised the hairs on the back of my neck. It sounded just like the harmony Rae had lost herself in hours before. When I noticed a guitar case sticking out of the man's cart, I ran to my car and sped to the hotel.

I left the radio turned off.

In the weeks since, echoes of the busker's song have haunted me. The melody is seared into my brain. I hear it everywhere I go – lurking in the hook of my favourite song, concealed between notes in an elevator, drifting onto the sidewalk from a café, a commercial jingle, my ringtone... Each time a melody sends prickles up the back of my neck, I check that my shadow's in place, that a pale faced man in a bad suit isn't pursuing me.

I'm ashamed to admit, but while I watched that disc burn, I only felt its loss. Despite what I'd witnessed, the fan in me, the collector and member of the metal community wanted to save it. Wanted to share with everyone what had happened that night in Austin.

Above all, heavy metal is a place for fans to vent, to say or sing or scream what we may be scared to admit, even to ourselves. At a show, surrounded by hundreds of people or alone at home with an album, metal connects us with others who've felt the way we do – who've fought with the shadows. I wanted to show them that the shadows are real, that our nightmares are real. I wanted to show everyone how Sam Garber stood defiant, bass in hand, unbowed by the shadows beyond even the point where her body gave up.

Lily Nobel

The Making of Planet Earth (2006) Ep. 11

We are inside the stomach of the submarine, feeling the weight of the Atlantic. This is not unlike one of us being inside of the other's body and vice versa. We are going down to the bottom of the ocean.

And, for some reason, Elle is here too. Like a grisly section from a piece of meat you've bitten into and now can't stop chewing on. She does not move how we do, does not feel in her own muscles the stir of the creatures outside of the submarine's hull. The cameras and controls are not extensions of herself. The monitors that show the growing dark as we move too deep for sunlight are not her eyes. She fears the mounting pressure – she told us as much – but she cannot begin to imagine the weight.

Her orange hair in a bulging braid. The plumpness of her face, the summerish blue of her eyes like a domestic body of water. Like a swimming pool in a backyard in Florida, where she came from. She told us the day she was introduced as the third member of our crew that she was from there – she pronounced it *Flah-rid-a* – and that she had loved the ocean since she was a little girl. That's what they all say. We were embarrassed for her and by her. Her delicate, painted fingernails. Peach pink. We watched our producers watch her like charmed mothers.

There is a type of sea bird that only eats bait fish that flicker in schools like light on the waves. The birds cannot dive deep enough to get the fish on their own. They don't have the lung capacity inside their ballooning, ruffled chests. So the birds must wait until dolphins with their skill, their muscled silver bodies, drive the fish closer to the surface for their own meal. Only then can the birds dive in to get them, still struggling all the way down.

Elle said she'd loved the ocean since she was a little girl, but she'd only known the tangles of the Everglades. We came to associate her with those miniscule estuary ecosystems. Roots that can be torn out by storms and boats. Alligators are killed by hunters, bolts ripping through the crust of their scales. Bodies coincidentally mangled by tour boats weighed down by fat, sticky tourists. Those fragile lizards are the best beasts the freshwater has to offer. Children dive down and touch the bottom of these bays, only seconds under the water, digging their hands in the lukewarm muck.

It has been days and we have not reached the bottom of the ocean. Not even close.

When we are not getting footage and maintaining data, we have taken to sitting separately in the two rooms of the submarine and feeling the pull towards each other through the walls. The descent pushes us inwards: the ocean wants to crush this metal body like a woman stomping a beer can into a silver quarter. We tell each other we can feel the bile wither inside of our livers.

Elle takes the measurements wrong. She is the human error in our box of perfect tools. She can't do *maths*, we sneer to each other. She's just graduated college, used to worlds of people telling you what you did wrong. Elle likes when people coax her through knowledge. This is not the world of the ocean. Not the world of the submarine. She watched the giant manta rays glide, but did not see how they guided mouthfuls of plankton and detritus through their frames with their massive exposed jaw bones.

She leaves herself Post-It notes everywhere like flakes of her dry skin. She tries to keep her brain taped together. There is nowhere to throw out her notes without her knowing where they've gone, so we just eat them. One of us chews them up, then passes it through her mouth for the other to swallow.

Today, Elle got footage of a sawtooth eel hanging still in the water like a belt from a coat hanger. She kept the submarine perfectly still with one set of controls while guiding the arm of the camera slow enough not to startle the eel. She thinks she is learning. She wants us to tell her she's doing better.

Tonight, we deleted the footage while she was asleep. One of us negotiated through the computer, her hands caressing the buttons, then the other sucked the taste of the machine from her fingers.

We haven't been sleeping in the stomach of the submarine because it would be uncanny to sleep apart, but when we are resting close together the urge to bleed through the bounds of the other's skin, to taste the other's sweat, to put the white part of our fingernails under the white part of the other's, is insufferable. It burns like trying to keep the lid on a pot of boiling water with your bare hands. So we just do our duties in the submarine all night and day, talking like people talk, brushing past each other like any person might brush past another.

We woke her up just before 5 a.m. to tell her there had been a malfunction and her footage of the eel had been deleted. There were dry yellow particles on the inside corners of her eyes and around the edges of her mouth. She cried and tried to hide it from us. We watched her.

Sometimes, we want to fuck her. We think about how we could make her desire us, but the idea has little sway. We want to hook our fingers around her bottom teeth, though, and drag her around like a fish we've caught. That is the way she is pretty to us. We are not *pretty* to each other. To each other, we are like the weight of the dark of the sea so many miles down.

One of us is older. Her hair is black, but starting to cut through with single threads of grey. She's worked in the ocean for a long time, longer than the other has been alive. She knows the size of things – how the biggest fish is a 30 ton whale shark, how at the bottom the isopods like giant woodlice are a third of a metre long. She says she can feel the scale of the ocean with her entire body. Says it pulls her apart from herself.

The other is young. She knows the balances of things. Black sulphide, she says, feeds the ecosystems. She knows how creatures must conserve energy, how they idle, how they eat each other. Says the nautilus only eats once a month, says the monkfish is perfectly still for days waiting for a meal. Her own body is thin and small.

One of us said the only time she'd orgasmed in her entire life was when the current had swept her away from the beach and she'd felt the water fill her throat, so the other held her head underwater for almost longer than she could stand when we were in the diving pool training for our journey into the sea. But that was only in the dive centre, with the yellowed walls, the echoing ceiling patterned with the reflection of sunlight off the water, so it hadn't done anything but make her hungrier.

The temperature falls. The submarine passes by zones of strange creatures that captivate Elle. That's what she says – they're *captivating*. She gazes out of the monitor with her unbelievable foolish eyes. We mock her to her face. Of course, we say. They glow. They move without moving. They dance like dancers dance. They'd eat you, your soft body. Even the small ones could do it, come in through your orifices and eat particle by particle so carefully you wouldn't feel it. But they'd be breaking you down. And the big ones – it makes us laugh to say this – they wouldn't even notice you. You would not be worth the energy it would take to eat you. We watch her fold back on herself, away from us, but wherever she goes she is inside the submarine, which is our body as much as our own bodies are.

We remember the day she trained with us at the diver centre, how we could see hair she missed shaving on the inside of her thighs. We pointed it out quietly to our instructor, a woman a little older than both of us, and she'd been amused too. Elle doesn't understand. Both of us, and the dive instructor, and the women on the production team – the kind of people we are, our knowledge, our drive towards the deep, our metal bodies. We are all camera and muscle. Submarine and salty sweat.

Today, the submarine passed by one of those towers of tube worms feeding off a volcanic vent. The ends of them, the mouths, looked like the openings of vulva. We said this to Elle. She looked away. We pinch each other until there are tiny spots of blood, then suck on the openings and spit the liquid out on the ground and walls. It looks like rust when it dries.

On the seafloor there are entire ecosystems nourished by the bodies of dead whales. By the time they reach those depths, their skin is pallid and malleable. The crabs, the isopods, the sea urchins, they tear the corpses apart. They digest the tissue, fuck in their indeterminate sea creature ways, and have chitin children that will live in the bones of this dead thing, waiting their whole lives for another, perfectly still in the dark. Oh, those heavy mouthfuls of whale. The giant, limp creatures' silent, dead descent.

The Earth is two-thirds water. 90% of the living space is here in the oceans. Our mother, the Atlantic. Each moment we descend, we feel the same thrill the crabs feel when they finally dig into the whales. Even the tiny creatures, you know, feed off of dead things from higher up – they call the tiny particles of flesh marine snow. Smaller than you can see, picking through unfathomably light touches of sustenance.

Elle watches us. Her freshwater eyes. She tries to stay away but thinks about us all the time. We think she might be jealous. We caress the cameras, steer the vessel. We are going down, down, down, to the floor of the ocean, where the pressure is three hundred times greater than anyone else on Earth will ever feel.

Scott Beggs

The Starving Feeling

I'm placing the finishing touches on my playground schematic when dad's knee slams into mine and my stylus slips. His knees feel thin, and they hit hard enough that I think he might have Disengaged, but his eyes stay closed, and he lifts his hand to toast an invisible glass of champagne to a roomful of people I can't see.

His room at Bright Hill is about the size of my dorm room back at Baylor, a fact that they advertised as a plus. Residents are encouraged to socialise. Bingo. Something called canasta. The corridors are always quiet. I never hear anyone call out B4 or N39.

With his arm raised, I wait to see where he puts his other hand. On the heart means he's Engaging with his worm to relive his 20th anniversary party. Small salute means retirement gala.

He pats his chest lightly and takes a sip from a glass only he can see. The flavours no doubt swirling in his mouth like expired magic. I try to think of my own memories of the party but come up short. What I wore. What finger foods I spit into my napkin. The details won't come. I know my worm will have them, but the thought of Engaging next to dad depresses me, and I slump in my chair thinking about what we might have looked like if I shut my eyes and disappeared next to him. Two men reliving the same evening, minds apart, knees touching.

My heart turns to brick. I want nothing more than for him to open his eyes and see me. I ctrl+z the stray mark on the schematic and turn back to my tablet.

The squeaky wheel of a cleaning cart gets louder in the hallway and clangs to a halt outside. Nelelli Marie knocks and walks in before I can answer, tossing a roll of toilet paper at me.

'You're welcome, Mr Womble.'

'Jayson.'

'Alright, alright, Mr Womble. Stop flirting,' she says, bone dry.

I roll my eyes and place the toilet paper on the floor by my side. In my head I'm feeling clouds and cotton powder.

'Thank you, Nelelli.'

'Don't thank me until you use it. One ply. Everything here is the very best from the lowest bidder 'cause no one needs this stuff anymore.'

'I'm sure it'll work fine.'

She looks at dad raising his unseen glass.

'I'll never get used to that,' she says, leaning against the doorframe. She must be about ten years older than me, and she looks like she's propping the whole building up.

Bright green eyes and brown skin. 'I wonder if I fling my arms around like one of those inflatable tube guys when I'm Engaging. Maybe I should set up a camera. Whatcha think?'

I want her to leave. I imagine my father waking up with her there, my having to waste his fleeting moments of rare consciousness on shooing her away.

'You know my daughter is Bliss, so no judgement here,' she says, and I must look like a cartoon puppy because she furrows her brow and backtracks. 'Are you not Church of Bliss?'

I fake a chuckle and shake my head.

'The abstainers? Nope. I've had my worm since sophomore year,' I say, pointing to my gut. 'She's in there swimming laps as we speak.'

'Precious. Did you name her?'

'I hadn't thought to, but maybe I should,' I say. 'Like an old car.'

'I just never see you Engaging, and ev-er-ee-body who visits Engages. They want to say they showed up, you know? But they're all in those rooms, the ones that do come anyway, all zonked out. Flying off to God knows where.'

And I remember. Dad gave me a sip of champagne that night. I wouldn't shut up about it at the lunch table the next day. He smiled as the bubbles hit my nose, and the taste was crisp like lightning.

'Hold up. If you've got a worm, why'd you need toilet paper?' she asks.

'My boss is having a baby shower, and she wants to play an old-fashioned game where they see how many toilet paper squares it takes to wrap around her stomach.'

Nelelli laughs, and it sounds like coming inside from the cold.

'Do you want to sit?' I ask, giving up on dad at least for the afternoon.

I'm 7 years old, and dad is dropping a squirming shark into an Igloo cooler whose robin red paint has muddied with age. We can't see the shore. Dad's hands are wet and grimy and the smile on his face is the horizon. I've never been seasick, and I'm not today. Even though dad reeled in the shark, I keep saying that *we* caught it. He wraps his arm around my shoulder and tells everyone, *yeah, we caught it*. I am tugging at the line again, but it is heavy like we've captured an anchor. The sea air isn't as salty as I think it should be. I put on more sunscreen, and the creamy film irritates my skin to goose pimples and gets on the soggy ham sandwich we packed when I eat it faster than I mean to. I wipe my hands on my swim trunks and it comes off, all of it mayonnaise and sunscreen and a fleck of American cheese. I sunburn anyway.

I'm in the living room, curled up on a blanket spread out on the fraying carpet in front of the television, watching the hyper-intelligent cartoon rats of NIMH as a fan blows the aloe dry against my skin. My mother brings me a cool drink that fizzes. She air-kisses my forehead before leaving me to try to sleep. As I doze, I hear my father tell my mother in the kitchen, *you should have seen it, he was great, he caught it all by himself.*

I ingested my worm after the full length of both arms were tattooed, so the idea of getting something permanent wasn't that exotic. *Eucestoda Peritialis*. Some old guy in Sri Lanka found it in a swamp, I think. Or a grove. He started having outrageous waking dreams. Hallucinated his long-dead mother and ate her stewed eggplant. Didn't need to eat real food or shit or piss ever again. Thought he was a god.

The worm gave him all he needed, ate what he didn't, and let him plug into his own mind to build or remember his reality. Doctors gave it the irritating Latin name no one ever used, but kids in Sri Lanka call it *siyalla paṇuvā*. 'The everything worm.' So, we called it Silly or Perry when it was on the streets here, but it didn't stay there long. People wanted it, so people got it. The worm turned into Flexefen and Heliotropin righteously quick. Commercials with grinning actors in lab coats and everything. It's tough to go back to crawling after sprinting the infinite.

It can't put a roof over your head, though. Sometimes you see people on the street, eyes closed, living some sweet dream over and over again until the elements take them.

I went through the popular stages of learning to Engage just like most everybody. All the worldly delights. That Michelin three-star meal. The breakfast tacos at the place that shut down my senior year of high school. Sex with anyone in every way. Crushes and movie stars. Some people stay there forever, sunken eyes with fat bags as they mope through day jobs so they won't get evicted from having a safe place to disappear from this world. It's not like it gets old exactly. Not for me. I still return to the carnal all the time. Like apes with an orgasm button. But most everyone moves on to more complicated fantasies. Feeling the force of being sucked into a black hole without dying. Swimming the English Channel as a badger. Spending a year as an Elm tree.

Reliving your 20th anniversary party.

I don't blame my dad, but I wish I could.

My boss, Mrs Fichtner, has us meet at the Chuck E. Cheese during the day to 'make me see what we're up against,' so my car drives me over there while I Engage to listen to all of Chopin's études with a thousand ears, each sound swirling an abomination and careful sweetness gentle as rain into the soft parts of my soul. It's a single planet-sized cymbal crash and a trillion skipping tones harmony-laced in its coherence. It forces me to swoon. The call is strong, and my chest swells, or the chest as I imagine it does. The heart inside my brain pounds, happy and murderous. Filled with energy and ready to sleep.

Fichtner's hand-shaking paw is already out, stabbing at me when I climb from the car.

'Glad you could come in person. Feels like ye olden times! Let's go in and see the devastation for ourselves,' she says, already legs ahead of me, pregnant belly leading the charge.

The candy-coloured cavern inside is only missing the tumbleweeds. Not a child in sight. Huge light bulbs flash, all desperate to catch an eye. Torture-ready kiddie bops blare over crackling speakers hungry for any ear. In my head I'm feeling pizza grease and merry-go-rounds.

'And there you have it,' Mrs Fichtner says. 'I considered doing a PowerPoint but figured playing tour guide to the end of childhood would hit home harder. This is what we're facing. Congress will make it legal for elementary schoolers to get the worm when they vote next month, and this struggling former haven for miniature Neros will shutter along with...'

'I'm not doing a drum roll,' I say flat enough to hide my worry.

'...the playground you're futilely designing and into which I have put a large amount of the firm's development money. So, I would like to buy you a pitcher of beer, which I will have one glorious sip of in this melted Skittle hellhole while we brainstorm ways to pivot so the firm doesn't go bankrupt.'

'You can't have a unicorn without a horse,' I say.

Now *she* has the cartoon puppy look.

'Sorry. Just something that came to mind.'

'You're not stacking LSD again, are you?' Mrs Fichtner grins.

'Strictly off the clock, boss.'

'You're on the clock now. I'm gonna go see if that skee-ball machine still works.'

I'm several pours through the pitcher when the idea fully forms, so I speak my piece, wanting only to get out of there. Away from the colourful noise and musty scent of ion batteries and Kool-Aid. Back home where I can Engage. Or at Bright Hill where my dad might finally open his eyes long enough to take my hand, ask about my day, and listen like he used to.

'As far as we know, the worm uses our own mental capacity and understanding to form the experiences of our Engagement, right?' I say without waiting for an answer. 'We don't have access to anything outside the brain, so it's doing all of it. Sunbathing on Saturn is only how our brain *thinks* it would be like, and that's good enough to make it real. If a unicorn is just a horse with a horn on its head, you've gotta have a horse and a horn to make one, but what if you don't have a horse to start with?'

'Aw, honey. You're still trying to save the playground,' Mrs Fichtner says, tilting her heavy-haired head to the side.

'It's worth trying.'

'It's already gone. Give it up.'

In my head I'm thinking of Nelelli, pushing her cart, room to room, down a blank hall. Cleaning what's already been cleaned the day before. Turning the fleshy ragdolls so they don't get bedsores while doing Steve McQueen's motorcycle jump from *The Great Escape*. And I wonder what Nelelli sees when she is finally home with her eyes closed and mind ready.

'That's why it's worth fighting for,' I say without believing.

I pick up some Budweiser LSD at the Tiger Mart to stack with. The LSD means I have less control. I like that. Letting the worm ride my mind doesn't take effort, but sometimes I'd rather not know it's my mind creating the universe.

The dirt under my fingernails from my Irony Garden won't come out, but that's fine. It's all over my jeans, but I don't bother to brush it off when I walk inside, still holding the beet I've ripped from the ground. The trowel clatters in the kitchen sink. I wash and slice the beet, holding it in my hand like some ancient artefact ready for plundering. I take the bite, chew, and Engage.

I'm chewing a beet, its flesh peppery and mad. A delightful punch to the teeth.

I Disengage, and I'm chewing the garden beet, its flesh peppery and mad. Is it the same? Like, exactly the same? I Engage.

It's the same. Hardy as though there's dirt inside the skin. I Disengage.

And it's the same. Mostly. Maybe. Here in reality. There's something slightly acrid about the garden beet. I Engage and chew and Disengage and chew and Engage and chew. Yes, slightly different, but isn't every beet a little different from the last? Is the LSD hampering the worm from bitter perfection? The flavours linger, and I find I'm intensely hungry. A hollow suck in my stomach I haven't felt for years. Really felt. The starving feeling is sensational. All-consuming.

I realise I'm still Engaged, and my mind has invented the starvation. I Disengage and spit out my mouthful into the sink. My stomach is calm again. I look around the room, and my hands find the counter.

'I threw up all over the boat,' I'm telling Nelelli, and her laughter rings out warm and ghostly again. 'You've really never seen so much puke from such a small kid. Like, medical journals should have been contacted.'

She's sitting on dad's bed, smoking pot, and coughing with a big bright smile. I take a hit, and a soapy pressure builds behind my eyes. We've spent every afternoon for two weeks this way.

Dad's head wobbles in tiny circles.

'Oh, and I'm definitely losing my job,' I add. 'When kids can legally get the worm, it's game over. I convinced my boss to let me keep developing the playground at least until the vote.'

'Playgrounds are the best,' Nelelli croons. 'I used to walk across the top of the monkey bars like I was in the Olympics.'

'Amen. But mine ain't getting built. I made this whole speech about unicorns and how children need experiences in order to successfully Engage, but it's just a bandage on a sliced throat.'

'You can come work here with me,' she says. 'It's just mindless enough to be unfulfilling but active enough that you can't Engage your way through it.'

I chuckle and pass the joint.

'You're here all the time, anyway.' A machine kicks on somewhere in the building, and it seems to come alive with a fuzzy hum. Someone laughs from a few doors down, and for a beat my weed brain thinks it's the delayed echo of Nelelli's joy. She catches me looking at my father, and I must have a stupid wistful look crowning my face. In my head I'm feeling tiny violins and tissues.

'My pop cheated on my mom,' Nelelli says, as if reciting a quiz show answer.

'Oh, shit. I'm sorry.'

'Me too. It was for a long while, and he came to his senses at one point. She took him back, but it was always strange to see him walking around the house like nothing. Cocky son of a bitch, you know? I hated him for years until I kind of forgot to. He and mom had to come to a place like this. Not a good one. When I'd come to visit, they looked like they found something in each other, like they'd fallen for each other a second time. You know when you pull and pull and pull on a rubber band, and then it snaps back and stings your finger but just sits there on the table totally normal again? It was like that.'

I nod, looking everywhere but dad's closed eyes.

'I was always more like my mom, too,' she says. 'Her memory went first, which was such a shame because she'd sung all these fantastic disco hits as lullabies to us as kids, and I knew she'd never sing them again. I started humming them to her, and she'd say something harmless like, "that's nice", and then keep slipping away.'

Thin smoke rises from the joint trapped between her fingers.

'Then his memory started to go before she died. Those years – I mean. Fuck. I wouldn't wish them on my worst enemy. And then we buried her, but Pop couldn't remember, so he'd wander the halls in this ratty bathrobe we bought him for Christmas years back, shouting for her. He couldn't mourn because he didn't even know she was gone.'

'Did it get any better?'

'He eventually died.'

The halls are quiet. The humming and the laughter all gone.

'Can I hug you?' I ask, and she nods just enough, and I sink my face into her hair, too long since I've felt this.

'We naturally spend time and energy on the things we care about,' she says into my shoulder. 'It's hard to fake caring because we can't help but spend our time truthfully. At any rate, I know what it's like to be an orphan with parents, too.'

'He's never waking up, is he?' I ask mostly just to hear the words out loud. Nelelli gets that I don't want an answer, and I love her for it.

My newsfeed is dominated by stories of the vote. Images of protesting Church of Bliss members plaster the screen, their placards reading a dozen riffs on how the worm is Satan burrowing putrid hands of idleness into our souls. No argument here.

I toss my phone onto the couch and pop an expired mystery pill I find in the back of my linen closet before Engaging.

The weather is stifling, and my head is being chopped off by a guillotine. It rolls into a basket that's soft but too warm from the heat, and I feel a distinct sense of annoyance as I look up into the executioner's baby blues.

I'm a mathematical construct unconcerned with your mortal worries.

I am having not-awkward sex with my high school sweetheart on prom night, but this time when Ben Millfelt opens the door to find me buried fully under the sheets by her hips, I don't leave her alone in embarrassment to sob until she falls asleep. I stay with her, and it is sweet and loving and I cannot help but show I care. We fuck as champions with skills well beyond our years, and our promise of staying together after graduation isn't just something we say to be kind. We drink half the bottle of Spumante that dad gave me before the dance and sneak into the hotel pool at midnight.

I am Santa Claus delivering toys to all the celebrating households in the world in one night, jetting at hyper speeds to squish down unwashed chimneys and creep into locked doors to fling tinsel and tidings of great joy which I stuff into giant socks before slamming a glass of full fat milk and store-bought cookies. The world around me moves slow and I move fast, and these are the same thing. I am chucking coal through Tiny Tim's window when my internal SOS beeps on. The Bat Signal shines for Santa, and I Disengage, mouth still filmy with milk.

The vote's over. To no one's surprise, children can legally get the worm.

'It's a tough break,' Mrs Fichtner says as we tromp around the build site. Already flattened and graded. Refilled with nutrient-rich soil so the grass can grow back in the places we want it to.

'What are you going to do with the site?'

'It's not really ours. We're leasing it through a swap partnership, and there's a lot of contracts I don't fully understand that say it's ours to build on but not really ours. So, it'll probably be a parking lot.'

'About as useful as a playground. What if I bought it?'

'You've got twenty million stuffed in a mattress somewhere?'

'No. That was stupid.'

She pats my back.

'I get it. I really do.'

The site is ringed by houses, doors shut, blinds closed, and it's hard to tell what kind of life is inside.

'Do you have a name picked out yet?' I ask, eyes flicking towards her belly.

'We're still narrowing it down.'

'Well, I got whoever it is a little something.' I reach into my satchel and pull out the stuffed unicorn.

'Aww. Thanks. That's so sweet,' Mrs Fichtner says, squeezing it to her breast.

'Kid's gotta have something to play with.'

Dad's face is slack and easy, his eyelids papery underneath caterpillar eyebrows. His hair is thinner than it used to be, but not gone. His gut is bigger than it used to be, but his hands don't tremble. His smile is still the horizon. An orderly has bathed him, and I imagine it must be like washing the mannequins at Tussaud's before the thought is trapped and ejected from my brain for being too cruel.

'Sorry about your job,' Nelelli says, professional courtesy melted into something else.

'Thanks. I'll be alright.'

Dad raises his invisible glass to toast.

'I was the one that convinced him to get the worm,' I tell her. 'He was never the guy to get the newest gadget or anything. I think he's still playing 8 tracks in there right now. I think he was content, you know? After mom went, he just looked so tragic. We talked on the phone every day, and I could hear the *him* leaking out of his voice more and more every time. So, I begged him to get one.'

Dad takes a pantomime sip of something real, and I'm tearing up.

'He did what I asked, and I lost him.'

I place my hand on dad's chest, and his hand comes down on mine, patting softly. His eyelids flutter.

'Do you wanna hang out after you get out of here? Pretend to drink a cup of coffee or something?' I ask, wiping my wet cheek.

'Yeah, I'd love that,' Nelelli says.

'I know a vacant lot we can go sit in.'

She laughs warmly before leaving me alone.

And just as she steps out the door, dad's eyes open. He pats his pyjamas in twilight confusion while his eyes adjust, but when they land on my face he smiles broadly as though I'm still the little boy he's slipping some champagne. He takes my hand. Squeezes it.

'I was having the best dream, son.'

I am 7 years old. My heart is racing, and the thrum solidifies in my throat. I want his smile to last forever, and I know it can't, and it's like holding a cracked egg in my fist, and I know if I start crying, I'll never, ever stop.

'How long you been sitting there like a lump on a log?'

'Oh, just a little while,' I say, somehow holding steady. 'What were you dreaming about?'

'Your mother and I were cutting the cake at our anniversary party together, and the knife sliced through, but there seemed to be endless cake, so she put her head on my shoulder, and kept her hand on top of mine.'

'That sounds really nice, dad.' My face flushed and tightened.

'Whatcha got there?' he asks, pointing to my tablet.

'It's – ahem – a blueprint I drew for a playground.'

'Can I see it?' His voice is just as I remembered it. Like harp notes cooked over a campfire. He squares his eyes to the screen to investigate, nodding his head, and chuckling to himself.

'This is great, son. Bang up job. When are they building it?'

'Soon, dad. Really soon.'

He looks up into my eyes, and says, 'I'm so proud of you.'

'I love you, dad.'

'I love you, too, son. Always have. Always will.'

'I wish I didn't have to say goodbye.'

'Then stay awhile,' he says, standing up and stretching. 'Maybe we can rustle up a deck of cards and a cribbage board. You want a game with your old man?'

'More than anything in the world.'

'That's the spirit,' dad says. He slaps me on the shoulder, and I ignore the starving feeling in my gut long enough for it to go away.

Rebecca Weinert

Rent

There is a thing in my living room. It sits on the floor, folded in on itself, between the bookshelf and the curtain. I only noticed it weeks after the move, and I know that it wasn't there when I set up the furniture. Maybe it needed something to hide behind before it showed itself. I'm pretty sure it wanted to be seen.

I only noticed it when I sat in my armchair in the far corner, nose buried in a book for the first time since the move – there were so many boxes. I looked up from the page and there it was, dark eyes peeking through dark hair, fixed on me.

I wondered if I should move again, after that, but I couldn't afford it. So, I moved the chair instead and decided to leave it alone.

My days are filled with work and when I come home, there are bills waiting for me. The new job was supposed to cover them, but I realise now that I was being optimistic. The move was more about the new address anyway but besides that, things seemed to be even harder than before. All I got was a more expensive flat – and a roommate.

I take one of the bills with me as I walk through the flat, a cup of tea in hand, as if looking at the sum in a different spot might change the numbers. I stop at the living room window and look outside, across the blur of rooftops and streetlights and asphalt gleaming from the rain.

The sum is still the same, of course it is, and I sigh and take a sip of tea and wonder if it's too late to change paths and become an astronaut or something else fancy that might pay more.

The thing is looking at me, half-hidden behind the curtain, but I can feel its eyes on me.

'You could help, you know. If I can't pay, someone else will move in and they might only walk around naked.' I sound more accusatory than I intended. But if I get swallowed whole by a demon in the corner, at least I don't have to pay rent anymore. I should write down which of my friends I'd want to inherit my books, just in case. It wouldn't be an official testament because a solicitor costs money. An informal note has to be enough.

The thing blinks, and I wonder if this is the moment they show in horror movies, where the music culminates and the special effects kick in, but nothing happens.

I put the bill down on the windowsill, sigh, and head back to the kitchen. I'm sure there are some leftovers.

I come back later that night to get a book from my shelf. The bill's still there – I was half-hoping it might disappear and I could pretend it never existed, at least for a while – but that's not what makes me stop. There's a small bundle of notes, neatly stacked, and I think I might be hallucinating now. I count them and it's about a quarter of the bill's amount.

I look at the thing in the corner, unmoved, unchanged, and it stares back. There's a flicker in its face, for just a second, and it might be a blink or a wink or my feeble mind playing tricks on me. I decide it's the first, definitely not a wink. I prefer to believe that the thing in the corner is not flirting with me. And if I decided it was my mind's fault, that would raise a ton of other questions and I don't have time for that.

I lift the stack of notes. 'Thanks.' It still leaves a good chunk for me to pay but I suppose it's fair given the thing only lives in one corner of one room and I occupy the rest of the place. And I haven't seen it draw a bath yet.

I want to ask where it got the money – are there side hustles for demons? Maybe it's being paid for haunting me? Is there an agency that assigns demons to respective houses and flats and makes sure it's the right fit? – but I suppose we aren't deep enough into our acquaintanceship to discuss matters like that. I haven't even asked for its name, and I wonder if it thinks I'm rude.

'I'm Quinn,' I say and hold out my hand, but it doesn't shake it. Fair enough.

I decide to check in other places of the flat for potential dwellers but there's nothing in my closet or underneath my bed and there's no weird shadows when I close the shower curtain, so I suppose it's only the two of us. It's a shame, really, we might have been able to split the bills more evenly.

I wonder if I am the thing's landlord now and if it has to come to me if there's anything not to its liking with the corner that it chose to reside in. I doubt it signed a contract to live here – with anyone alive, at least – and wonder if I'm charging it too much rent. It's not that nice of a spot, after all. The wallpaper is a little wrinkly (I'm not too practised but I did my best) and I decide to put a painting of a landscape I bought years ago on the wall opposite its spot, so that it has something nice to look at. I hope it likes landscapes, so far it hasn't complained.

My friends insist on a housewarming party even though I only moved a couple of blocks and they all saw most of the place when they helped me carry in the boxes and furniture. I try to keep things in the kitchen, but they want "the full tour" and I cannot keep them away from the living room for too long.

We stop in front of the bookshelf when Susan insists on looking at *all* of the book titles and decides that sorting them by name instead of height makes much more sense and Dan helps her rearrange. I would have stopped them, maybe, probably, but I'm distracted. I steal a glance at the corner when they're not looking.

The thing is still there, crammed in its usual position, looking straight at me.

I wonder if the others could see it too, if only they knew where to look. But asking 'hey, do you see that creepy thing in the corner as well or am I just going crazy?' doesn't feel

like the right topic for a housewarming so I don't say anything and wait, but Susan is focused on pulling books off
the shelf and Dan is focused on holding them and Holly
just stands there, watching the two, sipping on her glass
of wine.

I wonder if I should bequeath my books to Susan, since
she's so obviously interested or if her obsession with *just the
right look* of the shelf is a reason against it. Maybe Dan's a
safer candidate. He just seems happy to be here.

'It's a nice painting,' Holly says and points her glass at
the landscape that I hung up for my roommate.

I shouldn't say that.

'Thanks,' I say, eyes immediately drifting back to the opposite corner. Holly's don't.

She steps closer to the painting and cocks her head to
the side. 'I didn't notice that at your old place.' It's a cheap
print of something that was in style maybe twenty years ago
and I got it for a few bucks at a flea market and never hung
it up. Holly's always kind.

She's not a reader, though. I might leave her something
else in my will. She'd appreciate that.

'I found it in the attic when I cleared out the space. Never
hung it until now.' I step next to her and wonder if I should
try and block her view of the corner or if I should direct her
gaze there instead. I end up doing neither. I wonder if this
is dangerous – if *it* is dangerous. If this night might go very
badly if I don't shoo everyone from the living room *now* and
pack my bags and leave this place forever. I don't suppose
you'd know that you're in the middle of a horror movie until
it's over, and even then.

Holly just nods and takes another measured sip of wine. She looks like a proper critic like this, her scarf still half slung around her neck and draping over her shoulder like they might dress the posh person in a movie. 'I don't suppose Josh would have liked it.'

It sounds like she's talking to herself but the name stings. I never told Holly, or the others, the whole story but it's the reason for the new address, the new job, the move.

She smiles, bright and fake. 'Not that it matters now. It's nice, I like it. Even though it's really off-centre.'

I have to agree, but this is the spot the thing looks at and that was more important than the centre of the wall or the rest of the furniture. Maybe I should have put some more thought into this.

I glance at the corner, catching the thing's glare. Its eyes are a little glassy but always focused, always *there*. There's a hint of colour on its cheek – what little I can see through the curtain of hair – and it's red and looks a lot like crusted blood.

I shiver and turn back to Holly. Maybe I'm making it all up. The urge to ask Holly to look at it grows, and she seems to notice because she looks at me and frowns. I want her to ask, I want her to take the first step, so I don't have to blurt out the question in the middle of niceties, but she shakes herself and smiles and says: 'It's cold, did someone open the window?'

I shake my head and I know it's the thing and I can feel that it knows that I know but before I can say anything, Holly says: 'I'd like some cake now.' And Susan and Dan abandon their half-finished project and follow her into the kitchen where the "Welcome Home Quin" cake is waiting, as if this place has been *someone's* home all along and I just happened to join them. I refuse to question why the baker was able to spell the beginning of my name correctly but not the end and then I wonder if demons eat cake or if there might be dietary restrictions to consider.

Maybe there are digestive reasons for only eating infants and blonde girls. I still refuse to drink oat milk because the texture makes my skin crawl so who am I to judge.

I take two pieces of cake into the living room after my friends are gone and put one of them down at the edge of the bookshelf, close enough to reach but not too close to be invasive. I sit down in my armchair where I can only see the cake and not the corner and pick at the bright blue frosting. It's raining again, the sky long dark and thick with clouds and the constant *pat-pat-pat* of the rain soothes my thoughts. I must have dozed off for a moment because when I look up, the plate is empty, only a handful of crumbs strewn on the carpet, and I feel oddly satisfied. I still have half a cake in the fridge, at least now I don't have to eat that all by myself and feel extra sad. It's a relief, really. And who knows, maybe there are vegetarian demons and horror movies just don't show that side of the experience. I wouldn't want this relationship to be hindered by stereotypes.

We get into some kind of routine, the thing and I; I cook and put a plate down for it and it's empty when I'm done eating. It doesn't speak, and I don't either, and it works for us. A month later, there's another stack of notes on the windowsill, the same amount as before, and I take it and thank the thing and keep my questions to myself.

Dan comes over for a drink at some point and sits down in the living room before I can stop him. He leans back in the armchair and looks straight ahead, frowning. 'What exactly are you supposed to look at from here?'

I shrug and sit down on the worn sofa, a hand-me-down that my uncle dug up online. I left the good one behind and I'd lie if I said I wasn't bitter about that. 'It's a reading chair, you're supposed to look at your book, not the nice view.' And I guess I could have angled it a bit more towards the window so I could look across the rooftops, or maybe towards the shelf to highlight the books, but it's facing the edge of the shelf, exactly as it covers the corner, the spot where I put down a plate every night. I don't remember if I put it like this from the beginning or if I slowly, unknowingly, inched towards this angle, towards *it*. I want Dan to lean over so he can peek past the shelf and into the corner. I want him not to do it.

I think I want to keep the thing to myself now that we're no longer strangers. Not anything else specifically either, but definitely not strangers. And I don't know what I'd do if someone else saw it.

Or if they didn't.

I shake my head and take a swig from my glass. Dan brought some new kind of beer that he wanted to try but it's sweet and sticky and I grimace.

'Josh asked about you,' Dan says, and I look up. The beer makes me nauseous, or maybe it's the mention of the name. Probably the latter. I take another swig.

Dan picks at the label on his bottle – he refused the glass – and I feel like he's avoiding my gaze. 'Wanted to know how you're doing. Where you moved to. Says you're dodging his calls.'

That's the truth, actually.

'What did you tell him?', I ask and wonder if I should have told my friends to keep my new flat a secret but that would lead to questions, and I'd rather pretend like none of it happened at all and that this is simply a fresh start for a fresh start's sake.

Dan shrugs. 'I thought, since you didn't invite him to the housewarming, you wouldn't want him to know. So, I told him to ask you.'

It's a relief, even if I feel a little silly since I only moved about two miles away, not two cities over, so the moment when I'll naturally run into Josh is somewhere in the not-so-distant future and I try my best to focus on the artificial strawberry taste of my drink instead.

I steer the conversation to other topics after that, and then Dan leaves and the flat feels a little emptier, a little darker. I go to the bookshelf, a glass of wine with me to wash down the aftertaste of fake strawberries, and let my fingers wander over the worn book spines.

I wish Dan hadn't reminded me of Josh. I wish no one would ever remind me of him ever again and that he'd just fall off the edge of the world tomorrow and take the past five years with him.

I look at the thing, wondering if I could offer it the half-empty beer bottle that Dan left in the kitchen. That might be pushing my luck, so I take another sip of wine and lean against the windowsill.

'Josh's an asshole,' I say because I feel like the thing is missing some context and when it doesn't react, only stares and stares and stares, I decide to fill in the gaps, starting right at the beginning. At some point, I get the wine bottle from the kitchen and abandon the glass and by the time I finish both the bottle and my rambling it's early morning but the thing never wavered, never moved.

I wait for a reaction, anything to show me that it understands that Josh is in fact an asshole, but all I get is a blink and I sigh and get up and drag myself to bed.

I'm not mad. We're only roommates after all.

A week passes and I forget about the evening, or maybe I suppress the memory, but I should have known it would come back to haunt me. It's Tuesday and I've just come home from work when the doorbell rings. I wonder if it's Susan, who asked me to borrow a book – or two, or three – less than an hour ago, but when I open the door, it's not Susan.

It's Josh.

I wonder if I can close the door again and pretend I never opened it. I don't suppose I have to worry about being rude after what happened. But I don't close the door, I just stand there and stare.

'Hi,' he says, shaking the rain from his hair. He looks exactly the same and of course he does, it's only been weeks and he's never been the "dye your hair purple to deal with your emotions" kind of person but you never know. I'm still surprised.

'How did you find me?', I want to ask but I'm not on the run and I didn't change my name, so I instead go for: 'What are you doing here?'

Josh grimaces and pushes his glasses a little higher, a clear sign he's nervous. 'I saw you last week and–'

'You followed me.' I don't even bother framing it like a question. Now would be the time to close the door. But he'd just ring again. And who knows how long he'd stay out here. I don't suppose one piece of cheese, stale toast and a handful of grapes could get me through a siege.

'I mean, I didn't *follow* you.' Josh scoffs. 'I just wanted to know... I mean, I *deserve* to know.' He leaves the sentence hanging. 'Maybe we shouldn't discuss this out here.' He glances to the neighbouring door and right when I say 'No', he pushes past me into the flat. And what am I supposed to do?

So, I follow him as he idles down the corridor like he owns the place and *I'm* the guest. He stops in the living room – why does everyone always stop in the living room? – and examines the walls and shelves like he's looking for something. He stops by the window, and I think, 'Now he has to see it, now he'll turn towards the corner,' and he's the last person I want to share this with, but he only looks at me, hands deep in his pockets, and this tension in his frame that I know from our fights.

'I'd like you to leave now,' I say. He stays where he is and I stay where I am, awkwardly by the door, arms wrapped around myself and wishing I had just closed the door immediately, no matter the consequences.

'How've you been doing?', he asks, and I almost laugh at the absurdity of the situation.

I sit down on the couch because I feel like this might take a while.

I can see the thing from here. It's staring at Josh, and I don't know why that makes me shiver more than having its eyes on me.

Josh doesn't notice. He scoffs and runs a hand through his hair. 'I feel like you didn't even give me a chance,' he says.

'Please, Josh,' I say, and a flicker runs through the thing, barely there and gone. It rears its head, just a little, the hair shifting to reveal more of its face, skin splattered red, gaping in places, crusted over in others. It stretches like a shadow, the body never leaving its place, only growing, growing, growing.

And my first thought is that I never wrote that note to give my books to Dan – or Susan – and that now it's too late. Josh is focused on me, and the thing reaches out of the corner with contorting limbs. And now he does look and there's a scream as the thing folds itself around him and pulls him into itself.

It takes a heartbeat, maybe two, but then it collapses again, and the shadow is gone. The thing is still sitting there, crammed into the small space, and now it's just the two of us and an empty space by the window.

There's a low sound, barely audible, like a sigh, and then its eyes fix on me and there's that blink again.

And I suppose I could afford to let it keep next month's rent. Now that we're friends.

James Everington

Self-Expression

Matt had only agreed to go to the art gallery because of a girl. He'd never met "Antonia", merely swiped right on her profile – a few messages later, she'd suggested they meet at the opening of an exhibition at somewhere called The Zone. Matt hadn't wanted to seem uncultured, and her profile pic had looked cute, so he'd agreed, assuming they'd go on for drinks somewhere afterwards. But as he'd gotten out of the taxi he felt nervous, not knowing if he'd be able to bluff his way through the evening. Matt knew nothing about art, not even what he liked. Still, Antonia's message had suggested there was normally free wine at these things.

Be 5 mins x she'd messaged him, just as he'd arrived ten fashionable minutes late. He'd thought an art gallery might be housed in an impressive building, but The Zone appeared to be just a converted office space, maybe once an estate agent or print shop. Frosted windows obscured the interior, although Matt could see weak lights and hear weaker voices from inside. A girl was standing at the doorway in a short black dress and holding a clipboard: Antonia had told him she'd put their names on the guest list. It was starting to rain and Antonia still hadn't arrived, so Matt walked up to the girl.

She smiled at him brightly and, as far as Matt could tell, genuinely – a genuineness rather undercut by the fact that pinned to her dress was an oversized and brightly coloured name-badge, like those worn by fast food workers. Except, when Matt got closer, he saw it read *My Name Is Unimportant*. He did a double-take: he'd assumed arty types would be all leftie and woke and even he could see the badge was demeaning. The girl had noticed his reaction and smiled in a conspiratorial way.

'It's part of the exhibition,' she said. 'You can buy it if you like. Five grand.'

'*Jesus*,' Matt said and she smiled again. 'Anyway... I'm on the guest list I think, I'm...'

'No need,' the girl said and angled the clipboard so he could see it; every line read *Your Name Is Unimportant*. 'Six grand,' the girl said.

'For a bloody clipboard?' he said incredulously, and was immediately afraid he'd shown himself up. But the girl didn't seem concerned; he guessed she was from some agency and knew as much about art as he did.

'What *is* your name?' he said. 'I'm Matt.'

'You're the first person to ask that! I'm not meant to tell... Stacey,' she added in a whisper, causing Matt to lean closer to hear. 'Hey,' she continued to whisper, 'maybe you could get me a glass of that free fizz in there and come talk to me later?'

'*Matt?*' someone questioned behind him.

He stepped back from Stacey quickly. 'Antonia?' he said to the girl behind him, sincerely unsure if it was the same person whose photo he'd liked online. She smiled uncertainly at him, and glanced at Stacey.

'I mean, yes,' Matt said. 'I am. Matt. Hey, our names aren't on the guest list but…,' he added, to explain both that he was in on the arty joke and why he'd been leaning so close to another woman. He realised his mistake when Antonia turned annoyed towards Stacey. Stacey smiled unconcerned (and more at Matt than Antonia) and showed Antonia the clipboard, repeating the ridiculous price tag. Antonia closed her mouth suddenly, looking nonplussed, as if she were the butt of a joke.

'Uh, shall we go inside?' Matt said quickly. As they did, he knew Stacey was looking towards him, and he had the ridiculous idea that she reminded him more of the girl he'd swiped right on than Antonia.

Inside, the gallery even more resembled an open-plan office, from which someone had removed the desks and company logo, but otherwise left untouched. The floor consisted of wiry, hardwearing carpet squares; the walls were faded off-white from lack of recent paint, holding up a ceiling of greyish suspended tiles, punctuated by square ceiling lights which either seemed to be off or flickering – surely not a good way to light pieces of art? Not that Matt could see any, anyway. It was packed with people, most stood in tight and specific clusters with their backs to Matt and Antonia;

presumably. they were looking at the artworks he couldn't see. And they were all voicing their opinions at once, for the gallery was filled with the hubbub of speech. Why wasn't *he* saying anything to Antonia, why weren't they moving forwards to see the exhibition? Matt wondered if Antonia was as intimidated by the art gallery as he was, and had only suggested it to impress him. He was on the verge of suggesting an alternative, more relaxed venue for their date, when a girl's features formed themselves from the crowd, and he and Antonia were offered the promised free wine. The waitress was dressed the same as Stacey, with the same "name" badge (did they cost five grand *each*, Matt wondered), and was similar facially, as if the exhibition's organisers had made a conscious effort to hire staff of the same "type".

'You don't look like your profile pic,' Antonia finally said.

'Oh, well, sorry,' Matt said.

'It's not a problem.' Antonia looked away from him and into the crowd; she drank quickly from her wine glass. The fingers of her other hand brushed his and he wasn't sure if it was deliberate or not. But, what could he have said or done to warrant it? He was hardly distinguishable by his looks, and since he'd met Antonia he'd barely spoken, and had been caught apparently flirting with the door staff.

'Well, let's go and look at the, uh...' Matt said, gesturing towards what looked like a painting, momentarily made visible by a gap in the crowd. He had been *hoping* for paintings, on the basis that even if he didn't know what they were meant to depict he could bluff his way through talking about colours and shades. As he and Antonia advanced, Matt was oddly relieved when people acknowledged his presence enough to stand aside for them; indeed, they seemed to positively shrink back, faces averted.

When they drew closer to the frame, Matt saw it was not a painting at all, but a mirror. And yet it couldn't actually be so, for the room it reflected, although accurate in dimensions and decor, was devoid of people, Matt and Antonia included. It must be a screen in the wooden frame, he realised, playing a video of The Zone recorded before anyone had arrived. Shot in some kind of ultra HD, since he couldn't see any pixelation at all.

'God,' Antonia whispered sarcastically as she pointed towards the title of the piece: *Vampyre*.

'A bit trite?' a reedy voice said behind them. Matt hadn't noticed anyone approaching due to the lack of people in the "mirror". He turned and saw a small man in a shabby black suit that seemed to hang from his frame; his eyes darted and rolled without meeting Matt's gaze once. Matt felt an instant dislike for the man although he couldn't exactly say why; his distaste felt like something thrust into his thoughts before the man had spoken, before Matt had even realised he was present.

'I mean, "Vampyre", really', the man was saying. 'Swishing around haughtily, stuffed full of tradition and desire – what kind of monster is that?'

'I dunno, you could be one for all I know,' Matt said, gesturing towards the blank mirror.

'As could you,' the man said, 'after all, you did have to be invited inside.'

'But there were no names on the guest list,' Matt said, wondering why his tone was so antagonistic.

'Oh, but you were still invited,' the man said.

'Are you an artist?' Antonia cut in to ask. The man flinched as if she'd shoved a crucifix in his face.

'Ah, no,' he said. 'We don't use that word here. I am one of the organisers, and if that sometimes involves getting my hands dirty and creating then so be it. But all our pieces could be created by anyone; none of *us* are important. Although sometimes some damnable self-expression does seep in.'

Maybe I was right to dislike him, Matt thought. But surely not to this intensity; the antipathy seemed like a foreign object, lodged in his thoughts.

'But don't let me dissuade you,' the man continued, his voice quavering but still managing a sneer. 'Try and express what *Vampyre* means to you if you want. Or just enjoy the free wine.' As if he'd conjured her up, he stepped back to allow one of the black-clad waitresses forward, a tray of full, sparkling glasses held out. Antonia took one and peered back at the "mirror", like she expected its missing reflections to have appeared while they hadn't been looking.

'What *do* you think it means?' she said, as if taking the man's parting words as a challenge. Gamely, Matt looked again, although of course there was nothing to see. What to say? Vampires were monsters, obviously. Had the artist meant there were no real monsters but people – but how could that be, when people were precisely what was missing from it? Still, he felt like he had to speak.

'Uh, there are no monsters but people. Us,' he said, regretting the words as soon as he'd uttered them. Antonia stared at him but didn't reply, and he gulped his wine (flat and warm already) and felt a blush shame his face. He looked away from Antonia, back to the screen: its image was still devoid of people but darkened, as if The Zone's shadowed spaces had expanded.

'Maybe it is about monsters,' Antonia was saying. 'That we can never see the real monsters, never know them because the one thing they aren't are civilised people at an art gallery.'

And for a moment, just for a moment, Matt thought he saw something *move* in the image. Not at a single point, but in a way he couldn't define, he saw a movement across all of the darkened space of The Zone, which was nevertheless the movement of a single thing... although the screen still showed nothing other than an empty and shadowed space. And like his antipathy towards the man earlier, the idea of movement seemed not to be quite his *own* thought but...

'Or maybe it's just crap,' Antonia said. 'Maybe it means bob all.' Matt glanced at her, saw she was smiling, and what he'd been thinking slipped from his thoughts like something too big to hold. He felt oddly blank, his more normal frame of mind taking a moment to return. Antonia glanced at *Vampyre* again, as if reluctant to accept her own conclusion.

'Hey, don't sweat it,' he said. 'It might all be crap in here. Let's just have fun, huh? We can just leave if you want.'

'Still, we should at least see more than one piece,' Antonia said. 'I've had more glasses of wine than I've seen pieces of art.'

The number of people in the gallery made it difficult to see where the other pieces might be. Matt found his eyes drawn to the crowd itself – not because of any interest or flamboyance within it, but precisely due to the absence of such things. Other than Antonia at his side, he found it hard to recall or distinguish other individuals within The Zone: he couldn't identify, for definite, the man who had spoken to them, but it was hard not to spot several drab figures that *might* be him. Similarly, Matt would look at a woman's face, glance away, then be unable to pick her out from the crowd with any certainty seconds later...

'C'mon,' Antonia said, touching his hand briefly as she pushed on. He almost warned her not to, as if she'd become indistinguishable herself. Matt wondered at his thoughts; he didn't feel himself. He wasn't used to sparkling wine. Antonia seemed even drunker than him, yet she confidently led him forwards. He felt himself swallowed up, and oddly disorientated in the relatively small open-plan room, as Antonia bobbed and swerved through the channels the gaps in the crowd created, and they reached another piece.

So You Think You're Special?

Again, it wasn't a painting but something electronic, engineered rather than inspired. Wires and antennae stuck out from another screen, this one black and with flickering horizontal lines like an old computer terminal. It displayed only text, in the digital font of an old LCD watch. Towards the top were the words *World Population* and a figure in the billions climbing restlessly upwards. The digits shimmered and blurred, as if the number wasn't just increasing based on some approximate computation, but was literally keeping pace with every human birth and death.

The bottom half of the screen similarly displayed text – descriptions of everyday activities – and a number. Both changed continuously. As Matt watched, it said *sleeping;*

then *eating + drinking*; then *defecating/urinating; hailing a taxi; ending an affair; showering or bathing; failing a job in-terview...* It was almost impossible to make out the precise number for any category, each count blurred by so quickly. Deciphering the numbers was made even harder by the fact the lower corner of the screen seemed smeared in dried brownish blood or shit.

Holding hands: 5,064...

The whole display was very hot, so much so that Matt found it hard to stand close to it.

Hearing a diagnosis of skin cancer: 3..., ...

God, what am I going to say about this *one?* Matt wondered. His thoughts felt emptied, his mind open-plan.

Drinking insufficiently chilled white wine: 2..., ...

'You see, art does tell us truths!' he said too eagerly, turning to raise his glass to Antonia. Because he was facing her he didn't notice what the display said next, but her expression grew tense and, without looking towards him, she jerked out her hand and gripped his painfully.

Matt turned back to the screen, but only saw the words *...in black...* before they changed again, replaced by *stamping on an earwig,* but he was already thinking about Stacey in her black tight dress and then he was...

eating while crying

...thinking about nothing, just seeing a darkness, the blank darkness of his thoughts...

tearing up a manila envelope

... or were they his thoughts at all because couldn't he see *himself* in that blackness, as if objectively outside himself, and for...

fantasising about fucking a girl who isn't

...away from himself in that...

'I said I don't like it!' Antonia repeated, loudly – he'd been aware of the fact she'd been speaking but had been so absent from himself he'd not comprehended. Matt blinked; his thoughts were like fragmented things in the air around him and he had to struggle to bring them together again. Antonia was glaring at him. She must have given her wine glass to one of the staff since both her hands were bunched tightly together at her sides. Matt realised his own glass was gone, too, even as he couldn't remember anyone having taken it.

'Look, I'm uh, sorry,' he said to Antonia, although he couldn't have said for what. He felt uneasy, on edge like he sometimes did at home if he'd smoked enough to give himself the fear and every noise of his settling house became the sound of intrusion. The noise in The Zone, the accumulation of everyone's opinions and self-expression being voiced grated on his nerves (despite not being able to make out a single distinct word), yet what was at risk of intrusion here?

'Can we just go somewhere...' Antonia started to say.

Were they all saying the same thing, Matt suddenly wondered. In different rhythms, with different inflections and accents, but was *everyone* in the gallery saying fundamentally the same...

'And what do you think of this one?' a low voice said in his ear, making him jump. He heard Antonia swear under her breath.

Matt couldn't be certain it was the same man as before or not. *Face blindness*, he thought, *that's a thing isn't it, but can it really come on so suddenly?* And it wasn't like he couldn't distinguish individual features, just they slipped away, too unimportant to remember.

The man was still obviously awaiting a response.

'I think it's *crap*,' Antonia said. 'Soulless rubbish.'

'Oh soulless, yes,' the man said, so listlessly it seemed to take Antonia aback.

'Matt, can we *go...*'

'It made me think of darkness,' he heard himself interrupt her. 'It was moving, shifting...' He was speaking slowly, like someone in a foreign tongue trying to find the right words, and failing. 'But I don't know, I... well. Art has never... I didn't realise I had it in me,' he finished lamely. 'The darkness.' Why did he keep saying that word, like a scared child.

'I'm going to the bathroom,' Antonia said, looking around for it. She sounded annoyed, and Matt almost said something to detain her. Instead he watched as she pushed into the crowd and it was hard not to think she was being swallowed up by shadows – was black "in" among the art crowd then? – as people shifted to let her pass, shifted back to block his view. He thought that, rather than going to the toilets, she'd ended up in front of another artwork, with the dark crowd at her back.

'Why,' the man said quietly, making him jump, 'do you think what you saw had anything to do with *you?*'

'With *me?*' Matt said, turning back to the man in annoyance. 'Look, just because I didn't go to university or some posh art school or, or... It doesn't mean, what I *mean* is, my thoughts on it are worth as much as anyone else's!' He drank his wine to hide how flustered he felt – when had someone given him another glass? He vaguely remembered a figure in black, face blurred to his sight as if black-veiled, handing him a glass, but when he tried to place it the memory shaded into others.

'Or as little,' the man replied softly (Matt had the strange idea someone behind him had spoken and the man had merely mouthed the words). 'On that we actually agree with you.'

'We?' Matt echoed.

'Oh yes. We.' And Matt distinctly saw one of the waitresses mouthing 'we' as she looked over at him. Half the people in the room seemed to be looking over at him.

And then it was like his ears popped, for he couldn't hear what the man was saying at all, he was speaking so quietly, and of course if a waitress had glanced at him it was to see if he needed a refill, and everyone else was just minding their own business.

'I'm just going to find my, uh, date,' he said, and the man looked at him oddly, as if he were someone different and they hadn't just been talking, and looking at his face Matt couldn't be convinced that wasn't the case.

Despite The Zone being small, Matt still couldn't find Antonia. He wondered how many glasses he'd drunk, for as he moved through the crowd the faces that turned towards him were blurred and merged in his vision. Was he certain he'd recognise Antonia even if he did find her, in the state he was in? He said her name questioningly to a few of the smeared and smiling faces of the crowd. His head ached and he caught himself thinking thoughts he didn't understand and that didn't seem quite his, like when you snap back to alertness after half dozing off. He wafted his hands (someone had evidently taken his empty glass) as if to ward off intrusive, invasive insects swarming his head.

Had Antonia left, was this date that much of a wash-out? He could see the door to the street, and the thought of fresh air suddenly appealed. Also, hadn't he promised Stacey he'd filch her a drink? Matt took two glasses from the next indistinct server who moved by, and headed towards the exit. Although his perception of those he passed was blurred, he could navigate the room itself perfectly, it was locked soberly in place in his vision.

Stepping outside, he was relieved to note he recognised Stacey straight away; her face was clear in his sight, as was her smile of recognition. He dared to hope she wasn't just pleased because of the glass of wine. She stepped closer to him to take it.

'How is it in there?' she asked him. 'They haven't let me see any of it.'

'Uh, well,' Matt said. 'There was a mirror... well, a *screen*, I think, and a computer terminal...' Only now did he realise how few pieces of art he'd actually seen inside. Not just that he'd looked at so few, but he'd barely glimpsed any others in his peripheral vision.

'You know as little about art as me, huh?' Stacey was laughing at him.

'Listen, um,' he said. 'Have you seen my date leave? It's not going very well as you can probably guess!' His laugh felt as inauthentic as he'd found the crowd inside, but Stacey at least looked sympathetic.

'Oh poor you! I'm not sure, what did she look like again?'

'She, um, she has…' Matt started to stutter, and gulped at his wine to hide his confusion. What the hell did Antonia look like? He could recall her voice, the touch of her hand to his, but when he tried to picture her face all he could think of was a smear like an unclean lens, or a figure seen from a vast distance, her form just one among many; when he tried to recall what she'd been wearing all he could bring to mind was black. But he had to say something. He started to guess what she looked like, her hair colour, her complexion, her attire, until Stacey cut him off with a laugh.

'You sound like you're describing *me!*'

He didn't want that, didn't want any more confusion about who was who, and he blurted out 'no you're much prettier' before he realised what he was doing, then felt so ashamed he couldn't say anything else.

He was surprised when Stacey not only blushed as if in reflection of him, but stepped close to him again.

'Then why,' she said, 'are you talking to me about some other girl?'

'I, I dunno,' Matt said. And after all, hadn't Antonia probably already left? Even if she hadn't, she was obviously not missing his company or his incisive artistic commentary. Stacey was out of his league, surely – and yet, feeling like someone else, speaking another's words, he asked if she wanted to go for a drink with him.

'Now,' he added. 'Let's lose these arty types and go somewhere *now.* They've paid you up front, right? And no one is going to come this late surely?'

She looked at him, then smiled. 'Sure,' she said and Matt resisted the urge to make her repeat herself.

'Great! Where would you like...'

'Just one problem,' Stacey said, still smiling. She unpinned the badge from her breast. *My Name Is Not Important.* 'I can't just walk off with this or the clipboard, they're part of the show. Can you take them inside for me, give them to someone in charge?'

Possibly Stacey, being younger than him, wasn't much used to wine; before Matt went back inside she pinned the name badge to him, giggling as she did so.

His eyes likely needed to adjust after the bright street lights outside, the gallery was gloomy and murky to his vision as he reentered. Had someone turned more of the overhead lights off? A gallery surely should be well lit, but shadows seeped from the corners and the hems of the waitresses' black skirts (had they really been floor-length before?). Thoughts of his new date pushed Matt forwards into a crowd whose features he struggled to delineate, and he found himself face-to-face with his old one.

'Matt?' she said.

'Antonia?' he ventured, his confidence already wavering. Had she been wearing all black before? He couldn't remember.

'Nice name badge,' she said. 'Are you buying it?'

'God no, do you know how much it costs?' His voice sounded too loud; the other people in The Zone were talking, but hushed like when the lights dim before a show. 'I'm just, I, I'm just returning it...'

'For that girl outside? That's okay, I know you like her better than me.'

'What, I, no...'

'It's okay. Her or me, it doesn't matter. "You're not impor-tant",' she said, leaning forwards as if reading the name badge pinned to him; Matt started to correct her but when he looked he saw she was right. He blinked rapidly, trying to clear his vision of shadows. 'Shall I take it for you?' she was saying.

'No, I need to find someone who works here,' Matt said, but she reached out and pulled the badge from him, tearing a hole in his shirt in the process. Did she work here then? Blankly, he handed the clipboard to her, then looked to-wards the exit. He saw the door was closed, as if Stacey had shut it behind him, which at least explained the increased darkness inside.

'Before you go, take a look at one last piece,' she said. 'The one you missed when I went ahead.' So maybe it was Antonia after all? He wondered how long she'd been holding his hand, and when she had given him a glass of wine.

'Five minutes,' he said. 'Someone's waiting for me out-side, so five minutes.'

'Long enough.'

He had no idea what to say when he saw the artwork she led him to.

'Are they taking the piss?' he managed eventually. Even if he'd still been in the mood to impress, there was no way he could fake a personal response to *this*. What could there possibly be to say?

The piece was a small square of black paint, about the size of a postage stamp, smudged at the boundaries as if carelessly painted, even for something so pointless and skill-less in its execution. It had apparently been named *In The Art Gallery*. Matt started to turn away.

'Five minutes, you said,' a voice at his side whispered. 'That's what you said. Then you can take me on that date.' Someone's hand was grasping at his, but he was unclear whose; he shook his head to clear his vision from the smudged shadows closing in on either side. 'Just look,' someone was saying – man, woman, he couldn't tell. 'Look, think outside yourself. See outside yourself, your name is not important.'

'Pretentious bollocks,' Matt said under his breath, uncertain who he was replying to, but he did look at the picture, such as it was, again. Okay, he conceded, maybe it wasn't all the same shade of black, there was some minute definition to it. Or was that just in his drunken and shaded vision? He peered closer.

Was there some skill to it, some human expression after all? Matt studied the tiny gradations of darkness across the piece's tiny surface. He took a step closer to the painting, and it grew in his vision more than a single step would seem to allow for.

And then he reeled, clutched his head, (a glass shattered on the floor) closed his eyes. But he could still see the painting in the darkness there; the painting *was* the darkness there. In that darkness was the gallery, and within the gallery was that darkness. He did see himself from the outside, briefly and preposterously outside his self, but also unable to recognise himself for he was just one more body dressed in black in the crowd of people all dressed in black within the darkness which was within The Zone and which dwarfed and contained The Zone. He could still see the painting in the darkness there; the painting was the darkness there; and when he desperately opened his eyes, it was the darkness *there*, too.

But he knew what he'd seen after looking at the painting hadn't come from within him. Clutching his hands to his head had been pointless, because something had got inside regardless. The thoughts in his head were restless, a creature not yet fully settled into a new home. What he'd seen, what he'd felt – still saw and still felt – was pressing in from outside, belonging to some vast and eternally shrouded being, as indifferent to people as people were to a black swarm of midges. When it looked at them, it couldn't tell them apart. And now, with its alien and indifferent thoughts crowding out his own, neither could he.

Hands were holding him from either side now. He could hear words being spoken and feel his mouth moving and wasn't sure which caused the other. All his vision was the blackness of that single painting. Anything else – the lights of the gallery, the taste of wine in his mouth, the feeling of hands holding his, the possible shout of a clear and questioning voice outside – were just the faint and insignificant shapes within that blackness.

Matt blinked and smiled. He saw another person stepping down into the gallery.

He moved swiftly to intercept them, the better to offer them a free glass of wine.

Diana Powell

Haire

Beyond the furze, where she had come to, they caught the hares with dogs.

'*Furze-cat*,' the old woman said. 'Hunted for sport.'

She had seen it...

...gleaning motion wrapped in fur and sinew – gone! – chased by unanchored shades.

The hunkered men behind. Grinning.

Had seen it, too, with her own dogs.

They had brought the creature one morning, laid it at her feet, panting, salivating as they did so. A gift.

It had looked up at her, fixed.

Starer – another of its names.

She stared back, wanting to see it, but not wanting. A single drop of blood fell from its eye, matching the tear that fell from hers.

That was how she knew.

But not *when*.

She got rid of the dogs. It was easy enough. Rescue dogs, rescued again. Though she knew what they would be used for – it was there, in the eyes of the man who came to the door. Another grin, before he saw, and looked away.

And then she waited.

Upon arriving, she had taken down all the mirrors, or covered those fastened in place. She left the windows grimed and kept the curtains drawn, early and late. And she avoided shiny surfaces – glass-fronted cupboards, polished brass. Now, her hand reached to the corner of the towel draped over the bathroom cabinet, tugged, then stopped. No. It was foolishness. These things were done little by little. She must be patient.

On fine days, if she were strong enough, if she used sticks, she would walk towards the mountains, watching, looking for it, while knowing "it", she, wasn't ready, whatever it was.

Once, the hares danced round her. A sign, surely.

'Now?' she wondered. But still too soon.

The animals wove in, out, twisting, arched, reaching skywards, before rushing on. The early sun licked their fur, flecked their amber eyes.

She had danced like this. An abandon. Unfettered. No stylised steps, no practised movement. Her arms up, floating, her hips swaying, her head tilted back, eyes wide open. Her hair was part of the dance, yet had a life of its own, furling, unfurling. Round and round and round, in time with her whirling dress. A dervish. The strobing lights caught its gold. *Flame-leaper.*

The hare hadn't died straight away – the hare her dogs had brought. She had called them off, locked them outside, then knelt beside the animal. Already, it wasn't itself. The ears no longer stood erect. Instead, they fell loose over its face. Like hair. Hair/hare – the sound disturbed her. She found a box, placed it inside, on a soft blanket. The lustre of its coat had gone, too. Dull, instead. Its body had collapsed in on itself, wasted, while its movements were reduced to no more than an occasional stutter.

Everything it was, lost. It looked at her again, then died. She was glad.

The old woman came and went. It was her cottage. 'Nan,' she said to call her. Was it her name? Or what she was... a grandmother? Or something else? She brought things. A bunch of carrots, the earth still on them. Leeks, cabbages. 'Make cawl from them.' Milk from the neighbouring farm. 'Fresh from the cow.' Some hedgerow flowers. Some herbs.

'Steep them, they will do you good.'

"Good" was why she had come here. Or to get "better", at least. Fresh air from the mountains; trees and meadows further down, a river twisting through them. Beauty. Nature. Peace – all those things that were "good" for you, said to make you better. The old woman and her offerings were something extra.

Nan wore her hair long, as she had always done before – and loose, always loose, never tied. It was the longest she'd seen... down to her slouching hips, spreading with them. It was strange in someone so old. She reached out to touch it. It had nothing of the softness, the silkiness that hers had had. And the colour was washed out of it. But. Still. The woman let her be.

'It used to be the same colour as yours,' she said. 'Gold.'

How did she know?

The hair. The herbs. The hares. Was Nan a witch, she wondered? And the way she appeared, as if out of nowhere. What did her potions "doing good" mean? If she drank enough, would they make it happen? She drank some more.

Signs of spring appeared.

She could walk further now, without sticks, sometimes, above the gorse, not far from where the mountains opened out in front of her. There were more hares, here, as if, perhaps, they came down from the hidden cwm that lay ahead. Sometimes, she saw their mating – the bucks fighting for the doe. The chase. Oh, the pleasure of it!

It had been the same for her. Always, the men after her, not able to stop themselves, her, not wanting to stop them. Wanton.

It was the same when she fucked. The joy of it.

Like her dancing, her hair was a part of the sex. Her man – whichever man – loved it. The way she wrapped it round him, teased him with it. Stroked him. The two of them lost in it, tangled, revelling. Ecstasy.

The men, here, if she met them, lowered their eyes. *Scare-the-man* – another name.

They did not know what she was.

She did not know what she was.

It wasn't only her hair that was gone.

The shape of her body, its curves, its fullness, the secret places between the cushioned flesh; the slick of her skin. Her poise. All gone.

Bits of her, inside, had been taken away. Unlike her hair, they would never grow back. Parts of her "self", too. They hadn't told her this. Spirit. Joy. Lust. "Her".

That was another reason for coming here – to hide herself away. Somewhere in the middle of nowhere, where no-one would see her, would know what she had been. She hadn't known about the men.

She would go out at night, she thought, thinking to avoid them, to see the hares gaze at the moon, perhaps – or sing. Singing – was it hares that did that? But gazing, certainly. The moon lit her way through the trees. Only... it wasn't the moon, it was a lamp the men had lit, to draw the hares, to kill them. She heard the animal screams, the men's laughter. She hurried back indoors.

Higher up, when she could reach it, pausing to gather her breath every few steps, she began to see the young hares about the place, the smallest crouched in their forms, those older racing about, playing. 'Leverets', she remembered. One day, out early, she came across a feeding mother. A mother and child. The suckling. Sucking. Something else she would not share.

The season moved on. There were more young, litter after litter. It was what they did.

Nan brought something else, along with her vegetables, herbs, milk – stories. Tales about the hares. Saints and sinners mixed together, goddesses, devils; this country, that. The names of the creatures. Weaving the words around her.

Dew-hopper

    Corn-dweller

Grass cropper

    Racer – racing the wind, leaping the hedges, hiding in the ferns.

Wood-cat, furze-cat, witch's cat...

Witch, again.

        Was it some kind of spell?

        Was that what was happening?

        She listened, and learnt.

Easter came.

'Easter', she thought.

That was part of Nan's talk. Easter, Eostre, Ostara, ...a time of new beginnings, of change. The Sunday was the day of resurrection, after all.

Surely now.

She went out early, the dew still on the ground. Through the cleft in the crags of scree, she could see dawn breaking. The hares came down between the slopes, danced around her again. There were no men to be seen. God-fearing, perhaps. She took off her headscarf – the first time out of doors – and looked up at the rising sun.

She stood still and breathed, felt the sunlight reach down to her, the air go over her, then into her, reaching places she thought were gone. She drank the water of the morning dew through her skin.

And yes, she felt the slightest quickening inside, as if her blood was coursing through her once more; and when she touched her head, the tips of her fingers rubbed against... grazed...something – *stubble-stag*.

She breathed again. Deeply, easily, at last. Waiting... Waiting.

But there was little else. She went back home.

Another month went by.

May. More words untangled from Nan's stories – hadn't she said that the month's full moon was named for the hare?

To go out at dawn had been a mistake, if the hare belonged to the moon, not the sun. And yes, it was there, within it, if you looked closely. Not a man in the moon at all, but the shape of a hare. And wasn't it a creature that followed the lunar cycle, just as women did, just as she had once done, rejoicing in what it meant? So...

...she goes out at night again, as the moon is sinking down towards the earth, fuller, as it falls, the weight of it pulling it down. She slips through the trees, this time, away from the men, the lamps, the lights of their fag ends, the screams. Up, up, beyond the furze again, higher, finally breaking past the rising sides and entering the valley.

The moon hangs low before her, brighter, bigger than she has ever seen, the leporine image, distinct. And then, in front of her, she sees a circle of hares, looking inwards, at... what?

They turn when they hear her, then lope away – not in fear, she is sure, but as if they are leaving the place for her. She steps closer, to see what held them, and there, in the middle of the circle they had made, is a pool of water, with the shining disc of the moon trapped inside. Luminescent water, still as a... mirror.

She will turn, she thinks, she will go back; she is not ready to see. But the moon – the hares' moon – has led her here, they have given their sacred space to her. Another gift.

Hare, here, her. At last. Isn't this the time, the place where it will happen?

She moves forwards, just as a cloud drifts over, shrouding the top of the pool. Her body is there, its clear image laid out below her. And yes, her bones are fleshed, her limbs firm, curves round her into a woman's proud body, once more. She is, as she was, before the illness. Her "self", returned, reborn. Goddess.

She gazes up at the moon, to thank it, to praise it – per-haps she will dance to it! – and sees the cloud shredding, blowing away from the surface. And she looks back down, happy now, to see all of her, reflected, restored. Her sloe-eyes, her smooth, pillowed cheeks, her full lips, the smile playing around them; her resurgent locks. Her...

And sees...

      ...instead...

– in its stead –

  the head

of a

   hare.

       Shape-shifter.

David Hartley

Anima: Final Draft
by Sara T. Gravelly

–rossed the threshold and into her lovely house.

'I'm a hugger,' she said, extending her arms. 'Is that okay?'

She enveloped me and I did my best to reciprocate. She smelled of coffee and talcum powder, which was not altogether unpleasant. As we broke off, she took hold of my shoulders and fixed her gaze on mine. She didn't ask if intense eye-contact was okay, but we were through the looking glass now, I guess.

'I *loved* your novel, Sara. Truly. So please don't feel nervous. Don't feel like you need to impress me.' A squeeze, a slight shake. 'You've already done that with your words. Remarkable stuff.'

No doubt I was crimson, but I managed a smile and a small 'Thanks.'

'Shoes, if you don't mind. Just done the carpets.'

'Of course.' I fiddled at the laces and yanked my feet out, glad to be free of my boots after the long journey. For a moment, things felt fun, like I was visiting an old school friend.

'Come through.'

I glimpsed myself in the enormous hallway mirror as Linda led on. Thoroughly dishevelled. Sweat patches at the collar, dislodged tufts of hair. The tote bag with the gift made me look like some try-hard at a publisher's convention, not a soon-to-be-successful author. Linda, of course, was immaculate, as was her house. Not a thing out of place.

'We'll sit comfy, shall we?'

She led me into the living room. A plush sofa with a bazillion mismatched cushions faced a wall of floor-to-ceiling bookshelves. I marvelled at the books, as I always do. There was barely space to squeeze in a poetry pamphlet. It was wonderfully chaotic and colourful. The place, I thought, where life is. There was no TV, because there was no need for one.

'Here, here.'

She cleared some magazines from the armchair and ushered me to it. I sat and put the tote bag to one side, out of sight. In that moment, I decided against giving her the gift. It was a stupid idea that made me look desperate. I didn't need to endear her, she'd said so herself. So, the clothbound *Haunting of Hill House* would come back with me to Rotherham and restore itself in the collection. Probably for the best.

On the coffee table was a print-out of my manuscript. *Anima: Final Draft by Sara T. Gravelly*. Why had I put "Final Draft" on the same line as the title? It wasn't part of the title. Various coloured labels protruded from the sides.

'Don't worry about that,' said Linda, waving a hand over it like a soothsayer. 'Just a few quick thoughts to thrash through. We don't have to do it all today.'

'So weird to see it there,' I said.

'It's good, Sara, all good!' she said, leaning forwards and taking my hand. 'Listen. Take a moment right now to feel proud of yourself, yes?'

I nodded and tried to feel proud. 'Sure.'

'Yes?'

'Of course, of course.'

'Wonderful.'

She let go and sat back. I did the same, but the chair seemed to want to swallow me, so I edged forwards again. The tote bag thudded as it fell flat to the floor. Linda didn't seem to notice.

'Now then, all we're looking to do today is get to know each other a bit more, person to person. We can chat about *Anima* as well if we get time, but most importantly let's make sure we can work well together, okay? The client-agent relationship crumbles if we don't get on.'

'I'm sure it'll be great,' I said, meaning the relationship, but it sounded like I meant this meeting. Linda's smile seemed to hint that she was, as yet, unconvinced.

'Well, if I absolutely set your teeth on edge, Sara, then you have every right to turn me down and I promise I won't be offended.' She nodded at the manuscript. 'The book is more than good enough to scoop another agent if you decide to go in that direction and ultimately, it's your career, Sara, not mine. Is it *Sah-rah* or *Sare-ah*, sorry?'

'*Sah-rah*,' I said. 'Thanks for asking. Most people don't.'

'There you go, you see. Understanding. Mutual respect.' I laughed and she chuckled, and whatever ice remained was thawed. 'That's what I'm saying. That's what it's all about.'

'Sure. I'm excited. This is super exciting.'

'Wonderful. Now then, first things first, let me fix you a drink. Tea, coffee? Something harder, softer?'

'Oh no, just a tea please. Anything herbal, or...?'

'All the herbals you could shake a tit at, my dear, what's your poison?'

'I could murder a camomile.'

'So be it. I shall eviscerate a raspberry leaf, I think.' She launched herself up and strode to the door, then turned back and pointed straight at me. 'And I mean it, darling. The novel is marvellous. I've never read anything quite like it. Oh, and feel free to browse.'

She left and the room seemed to sigh with relief. Or perhaps that was just me. I took a moment to recalibrate my brain. It was happening. The last six years of my life validated. All those late nights, all those feeble excuses to get out of social stuff, all the arguments with Andrew. All worth it. I looked at the manuscript. *Never read anything quite like it*. I was still convinced it was as greedy as a parasitic wasp, with Shirley Jackson as its most notable victim.

She was just being nice. Buttering me up ahead of a gentle takedown when she reveals the vast extent of the edits. Or she'll drop the *unpublishable* bombshell and ask if I've got anything more palatable, which I absolutely did not. I looked at the bookshelves, stuffed to the gills. Imagined my hardback among them, as I'd done for so long. I still couldn't picture it. I frowned at myself. I got up and browsed.

And then I stopped browsing.

I took a step back, tried starting again. More methodical this time. Reading each spine, each author name. But no.

I did not recognise the books. Not a single one.

None of the authors nor the titles or any of the cover art. I was in bookshops and libraries all the time, I liked to think I knew most of the books out there. But this was...

It was as might be expected. Mostly regular paperbacks and various hardbacks that looked shop-bought or gifted. Nestled in there were some well-thumbed proof copies with holding covers, and a few ring-bound printouts that I took to be drafts. A section of the middle shelf above the fire-place held editions that look a bit more treasured – first printings, I assume, of books by Louise's clients. Multiple copies of a crime novel called *Blood Sugar* by an Eleanor McCarrey, and then a run of hardbacks of *The Atlantean Girls* by Samantha Sewelle. Face-out and proud at the end of the section were a trilogy of historical tomes by KH Stower titled *Remus Recalibrated*, *Romulan Restored*, and *Ruinous*. I hadn't researched Louise's clients, but that wasn't my fault. Her website had been under construction. Just her photo, an email address, and a brief summary of the kind of writing she was interested in. My kind of writing, I'd thought.

Worry fluttered at me as I hunted for names I recog-nised. Who was forensic scientist Dr OP Garrett? And the nature writer Polly Oldhouse? What were all these mystery novels by Van Broughton, who was the "must-read" sci-fi author Xi Yun? The publishing houses seemed right at least. The rippling waves of Pan Macmillan, the compass star of Gollancz, and plenty of waddling penguins on black and orange spines. But who the hell was Rebecca Rushton? Five of her books here and all were Penguin Classics. I pulled out the fattest one, *Drought*, and stared down at the cover. 'Timeless' said *The Guardian*, 'Essential reading' said the *Financial Times*. I opened the inside cover and skimmed the bio. *Rebecca Rushton, 1833–1878... the most beloved romantic writer of the period... novels and short stories have endured like no other... countless TV and film adaptations.* It listed her other works. *Colossus of Rhodes. Erudition. Making Time. Swift Swallow House.* Louise had them all.

I closed *Drought* and held it to my chest. I hurried along the rest of the shelves. Some titles were almost right. *Express Train to the Orient. The Secretive History.* There were detective novels by a Rankin but I pulled one out to reveal Fiona, not Ian. Plenty of myth retellings – Heracles, Pandora, Odin – but not against any names I knew, and I knew them all, some personally. Every nerve ending itched. I felt hollowed out. Was this a joke? An art installation? Had I gone mad?

Linda returned.

'Ah *Drought*,' she said. 'Can't do without it, can we?'

She passed me my tea. It was in one of those Penguin Classic mugs. *Golden Hour* by LJ Brickman. I put the

Rushton back. I took a sip. I worried the camomile would taste like liquorice or something, but it was right.

'So,' Linda said, moving close, 'where does *Anima* fit in there? Who do you put yourself with?'

I took another sip. It was too hot, scalding my lips. I turned away and crossed the room to seek out a coaster.

'Sorry, huge question,' Linda said at my back, 'but let's indulge. Let's get ambitious! You're in Forrest's and *Anima*'s there. It's a bestseller, 3-for-2. Who's it sitting next to?'

I sidled back to the shelves and pretended to look. 'Well, I er... I put it in Gothic New Weird. So, Nina Allan, maybe? Jeff VanderMeer and Aliya Whiteley.'

She frowned a little and shook her head. 'Who else? Think bigger.'

'Okay, well... Susan Hall. Shirley Jackson, of course. Du Maurier's the big one.'

'What's he written?'

I looked at her. No hint of a joke.

'She,' I said. 'Daphne du Maurier. She wrote *Rebecca*...?'

Linda cocked an eyebrow. Her friendly smile sank into a look that partly said *you're not getting what I mean* and partly *I think you're taking the piss*. She strode to the sofa and sat. She indicated the armchair, and I dutifully retook my seat. It was only when I bent my knees that I realised how wobbly they'd gone. A silence was deliberately left, so I filled it.

'There's a lot of *Rebecca* in *Anima*,' I said. 'Doppelgängers, the big house, the love affair.'

'Mmhmm.'

'But maybe it's closer in tone to *The Haunting of Hill House*. Did you see the Netflix adaptation?'

She broke off the eye contact and looked down at her hands. She twisted one of her bangles around to reveal sparkling jewels, then twisted it back. She cleared her throat.

'Sara,' she said, 'You need to calm down a bit, my love. This is a friendly meeting, everything is good. I liked your work, I genuinely did.'

I nodded. I wanted to say *sorry*, but my stomach chose that moment to roll and an acid rush of camomile tea shot up the back of my throat. I swallowed it, started coughing. Linda waited until I was done.

'You okay, hun?'

'I'm–' The sentiment died into another flurry of coughs. 'Sorry... Just a bit overexcited, I think.'

'I get it, I get it! Take your time. Just breathe...'

We shared a nervous laugh at that, and I made a show of taking calming breaths. So what if I didn't recognise her books? She was probably some sort of collector of obscure titles or something. She was bound to be more widely read than me. I turned a little to take the shelves further out of view.

'Sorry,' I muttered.

'Don't be,' said Linda. 'Don't be sorry, Sara. It's totally understandable. This is a big deal for you. Or it will be when I start shopping around this excellent book, yes? I am interested in representing you, okay? I hope you realise that?'

'Thanks.' Of course she was. She wouldn't have invited me otherwise.

'Okay,' she said, sitting back, drawing a line under all that silly *Rebecca* business. 'Let's talk *Anima*. Tell me how it came to be.'

How it came to be? On and off for six years in and around Andrew and Alfie. Furtive in the mornings like masturbation, or late at night like getting drunk alone. Deleting the whole thing in anger one bleak day in year three then paying some dick in Currys to retrieve it all four weeks later. Andrew telling me, with very little care, to sack it all in and put my energies into getting a promotion at work instead. Alfie calling it *Mum's time* in increasingly exasperated tones and then those long months of churning guilt when I wrote his worst habits into the demonic child character. Then the rest spooling out in the four months post-walkout on a creaky laptop in Kiera's spare room while she protected me from interruptions.

How it came to be? Maybe it came properly when I came properly, not with Andrew but with Ollie, Kiera's boyfriend, when she was away on that hen do. Maybe I had to seek the ending then because I couldn't cope with the crushing guilt, or the crashing desire to do it all again and again and again.

I said none of this to Linda. I stared at her as if trying to remember. And instead, I said, 'I brought you a present.'

'Oh?'

I'd annoyed her again. She didn't want a present. But it was too late. I retrieved the tote bag and took out the gift. The wrapping was immaculate. Gothic charcoal crepe paper bound by a silver ribbon. *The Haunting of Hill House* waited inside, a pristine edition.

'Just a little thing.'

'Well,' said Linda, taking it as if it were a court summons. 'Happy birthday to me.'

She cleared her throat and set to the unwrapping. The ribbon collapsed on itself, the folds of paper snapped up without tearing.

'You said you've never read it, so...'

She reached inside and pulled the book clear of the paper. She looked at it, then looked at me.

'I have read it, Sara.'

She held it up and I was pinned.

'I'm afraid this doesn't really endear me.'

A fresh first edition hardback of *Anima* by Sara T. Gravelly. The cover was a distorted angel made of twisted garden tools. The title enormous and embossed, my name emblazoned beneath. There were pull quotes at the top from other authors singing my praises.

Linda opened it and flicked through. When she reached the inside back page, she showed me the picture. Me, looking serious and just a little bit sexy, wearing a blazer and reclining on a leather armchair. The text below said I lived in Derbyshire with my husband and my son. I didn't live in Derbyshire. I lived in South Yorkshire.

'You've already published it?' she asked.

'I... I've not... I'm...'

The book was twice the size of the version of *Hill House* I'd wrapped. It had been the right size and weight when I passed it to her. Had she pulled some sort of trick, some sleight-of-hand?

'What's going on, Sara? I was very clear, I don't represent books that have already been published, including self-published.'

I would not have signed off on that gaudy cover. I would not have been happy with that author picture. I thought of Andrew and Alfie and an idyllic house in Derbyshire. I thought of Ollie and Alfie in a rundown council house in Derbyshire. I thought of a faceless man and a demon child in an entirely average terraced house in Derbyshire.

'What's happening?' I whispered.

'You tell me! You've come all this way. Haven't you?'

'I don't... I don't understand...'

She turned back to the book and sifted through the end pages. It didn't take her long to find the *Acknowledgements* page.

'"Most of all, massive thanks to my brilliant agent,"' – she paused, looked up at me, her fury barely contained – '"Linda Brierley."'

I was shaking. She must've been able to see that I was shaking. She snapped the book shut and placed it on the coffee table next to the *Final Draft*. I could not think of anything else to do so I snatched it and stuffed it back in the tote bag. In there, it would be *Hill House* again. It would forever be *Hill House*.

'Well,' she said. 'Is there an explanation?'

'These books. They're not real. They... they don't exist.'

'Which books?'

I couldn't look at them. I pointed behind.

'What on Earth are you talking about?'

'I think I should go.'

She tutted. 'It's a real shame, Sara. I was tremendously excited about this book. You're a fantastic writer. If indeed you've actually written the thing?'

'I really should go.'

'There were changes to be made, of course. I didn't care much for the ending. And that lengthy bit set in a swimming pool needed a lot of slicing down. Oh, and you have a nasty semicolon habit.'

'I'm going to go.'

'But, more importantly, you have no presence online, Sara. That's not good enough in today's world. You would need to promote the hell out of this book, or no one will get it. It's your story, yes?'

'I have to go.'

'Personal experience? We would have pushed that angle, that stuff fires people up. I might have even suggested taking the assault out of the final third and turning that into book two. Replace it with something less in-your-face. Something with an air of menace, you know?'

'Got to go.'

'But that's all academic now, isn't it?'

'Got to go.'

'Such a shame.'

'Got to–'

'Yes, yes, go on.'

I stood up. The handles of the tote were wrapped tight around my hands, strangling my fingers. I hadn't realised I was doing that. The weight was a light paperback, not a heavy hardback. I didn't look inside.

I hurried out, back to the hallway. My legs weren't working properly. I willed them on. I dared not look again in the mirror. I dared not glimpse the Derbyshire wife, the author mum.

It took me an insufferable age to get my boots back on. Strangled fingers, numb feet, boots that felt a size too small now. I didn't lace them. I heard Linda muttering to herself. I waited a minute, trying to hear. But I couldn't make out the words. She fell quiet. She didn't emerge from the room.

I opened the door as if sneaking out. Then wrenched it open and got the hell–

Elaine O'Connor

The Cure

Curing ringworm and shingles was a harmless enough vocation, but performing an exorcism was a different territory. News about the fella had reached Bagsy, like these things often did, via Alannah. His girlfriend had an uncanny ability to detect those in need of help, the desperate, the depressed, those for whom the last flicker of light in the world had been all but extinguished. Danny Maguire had been acting strange for a while, the wife had said. A sickness that no doctor could cure. Previously an affable and friendly man, he'd become withdrawn and quiet. Then the muttering had started, venomous curses and threats directed at nobody in particular but which were accompanied by a darkening of his eyes, almost shark-like. His voice took on a low guttural quality. Even Fr O'Toole had refused to help the man, petrified by the potential retaliation from the Antichrist himself.

Could the fella just be mentally ill, Bagsy wondered? Schizophrenia or that condition like the lad on *The Undateables* suffered from, where he shouted out random words, loudly and for no reason and without any control. Or maybe he was simply disco-damaged – word was that he'd been known to enjoy a night on the town in his day, quare fond of the auld yokes he was. But what if it really was demonic possession? And what if Bagsy was the only one who could help him?

Bagsy Mahoney was the seventh son of the seventh son and was presumed to have the cure. There were eight sons from three different women, little Jimmy arriving just six months after Bagsy, almost like a twin, but without the shared mother. Bagsy was not his given name, rather one which he inherited from his father, Ger "The Bag" Mahoney, a name derived from his role as caretaker of the local GAA team's kit. He transported them in a large canvas sack-like bag. Confusingly, each of Bagsy's seven brothers shared his nickname, but his requests to be referred to by his Christian name fell on deaf ears, and only the mother had ever called him Darren. Originality was not considered a virtue in the town of Ballyhooly.

Bagsy had always been sceptical about the existence of healing powers, as were Paul and Dermot, the two brothers with whom he shared a mother and a home. The Bag came and went as it suited, resurfacing only when the latest of his women had grown tired of his ways and sent him back to the wife.

'They're just jealous,' his Ma would snap when the brothers made fun of his alleged gift and taunted him with requests to fix the match score or replenish the empty biscuit jar.

'You'll find them when you grow,' she'd assured him, 'when you come of age,' refusing to relinquish dreams of the powers her youngest son might possess and the related respect and reverence she believed it would bring upon the family. But eighteen had come and gone and Bagsy had yet to feel any real powers beyond an ability to suffer through eight hours a day in Carroll's meat factory, chiselling through gristle and bone with a half-blunt buzz saw, before loading the severed fatty flesh onto a conveyor belt.

The years had drifted by and as it failed to materialise, talk of the cure had faded. The mother had passed when Bagsy was twenty-two – a fierce accident on the Tullow dual carriageway – and now, three years later, the only mention was the odd drunken dig from one of his brothers. This was how Alannah had come to learn of his gift. The pair of them had been enjoying pints with four of his seven brothers – a bag of Bagsies, as the locals called them when they went out en masse – when Dermot and Brendan had started with the slagging, asking him to turn water into wine, or beer if he could arrange that. Begrudgingly, and not without embarrassment, Bagsy was forced to explain to Alannah that he was the seventh son of the seventh son and how, on the day that he was born, the parish priest had placed a live worm in Bagsy's hand, and the worm had died. From that day forward, Bagsy's power to heal may as well have been written in the scriptures, only that he had never actually managed to cure anyone of anything. A load of old bollix as far as he was concerned. But he'd watched as the information registered and the euro signs spun in Alannah's eyes.

Alannah had been his girlfriend for a while now, though he wasn't quite sure how or when the status of their alliance had been cemented. He'd been getting the ride off her on a semi-regular basis, usually on a weekend night after several rounds of shots and when no other viable options presented themselves by closing time. Somehow, the arrangement had limped into relationship, not helped by a deep inertia on his own part, much like the job in Carroll's and the fact that, at twenty-five he still lived in the house where he'd been reared.

'Will you just see her?' pleaded Alannah, propping her chin up on her right hand next to him on the bed.

It had been a few months after she'd learned of the cure, during which time she'd been constantly at him with questions and uninvited observations designed to learn more about it. Not unlike his dearly departed mother, he knew that Alannah had a misguided belief that it would bring him, and herself by association, some sort of standing in the town. And his girlfriend had a nose for sniffing out money like a pig hunting truffles.

'I told you. My mother was deluded, God rest her soul. I don't have any fucking powers.'

'Ah Bags, go on, she's desperate like. Just try it. Didn't you cure me that time I was all but dyin' after Fran Carter's wedding?'

She stretched her right hand over to where he lay and dropped it suggestively on his stomach, slowly moving her hand down.

'You had a hangover, Alannah. And I'm fair certain it was the hair of the dog in the bottle of wine you drank that cured you,' he replied.

'There'd be money in it like, she'd pay.'

Alannah had a friend who had a cousin who was struggling to get pregnant. Two years, her and the husband had been trying. They'd done the free round of IVF, but nothing had come of it, and it had been suggested that Bagsy, being the seventh son of the seventh son who had a worm die in his hand on the day he was born, could assist.

'Jesus Alannah, I don't see how I can help the woman,' he said, sitting up and lighting a cigarette, wondering how, besides the obvious, he was expected to aid her in her quest to procreate. It seemed unlikely that this was what Alannah had in mind.

'I thought you were broke?' she said, pulling her face into a scowl.

She was right. Money had been tight. Bagsy lost three grand on a sure thing at the Galway races and the interest on the loan that he'd taken out to place the bet was racking up a lot faster than the horse he'd backed. Loan sharks were none too sympathetic to pleas about the cost-of-living crisis.

'I wouldn't know what to do, like,' he said, inhaling sharply on his cigarette.

Alannah had jumped to attention and pulled out her phone.

'I'll google it. There was a story in *The Mirror* about an auld fella up there in Donegal that heals. I'll see what he does. Probably place your hands on her stomach and say a prayer or something,' she said enthusiastically.

Christmas was coming and Alannah had her eye on a ring. She was living in fucking dreamland.

Reluctantly, he had agreed to a meeting and Jeanette Cowley, the woman looking to get herself knocked up, was summoned to the house. When the mother had died, Bagsy and Paul had inherited the house along with the mortgage. The Bag himself had been on the missing list for months, presumed to be shacked up with whatever poor woman had been unfortunate enough to be charmed into his affections this time.

From their research, prayer and holy water featured strongly in healings and the latter was promptly procured from Fr O'Toole, who had insisted he couldn't take payment – it would be a sin – but couldn't Bagsy buy him a couple of pints in Tully's that evening if he wanted to show his gratitude. In the front room of his childhood home, Bagsy lit three white candles, burned some clary sage and ran his fingers around the puckered, lumpy face of Jeanette Cowley, looking deep into her eyes. Next, he said a Hail Mary and a Glory Be – the only prayers he could remember all the words to. Truth be told, other than funerals and weddings, it had been some time since he'd gone to mass. Jeanette was instructed to close her eyes and Bagsy stood in front of her, sprinkling the holy water on her face while he recited a sort of spell that he'd found on Reddit by someone purporting to be a witch.

The fountain of life, the ever-flowing energy, bless Jeanette with a healthy child.

He felt like a right plank, and a fraud too, and vowed there and then that this would be the end of it.

Two months later, Jeanette arrived back at the house in floods of tears, pressing two fifty euro notes into his hand. She was pregnant. A woman from Athy with shingles came to him a short while later and, with some persuasion from Alannah, Bagsy performed another ritual. This time he lit green candles and read a passage from the Bible involving Jesus healing lepers. Sheila, that was the woman's name, looked a bit put out at being compared to a leper and he'd made a mental note not to use that passage again. Nonetheless, Sheila's shingles miraculously cleared up within weeks, surprising nobody more than Bagsy himself.

'A coincidence, Alannah,' he told her. 'Sure it had probably run its course.'

'And Jeanette? Even the IVF didn't work. And they'd been at it night and day for the last year. Bags, you have it, I knew it. You're a healer.'

He wasn't convinced. There would be some other explanation. Perhaps another man had assisted Jeannette in a more direct manner than Bagsy had.

Word of his "magic hands" spread. People spoke in hushed tones about the energy that he radiated. Bagsy didn't charge, but word got round that donations were appreciated. Some brought gifts, homemade cakes or farm produce and on one occasion, a bag of sausages – much to Alannah's annoyance. But many more dropped in cash and before he knew it, the loan shark had been paid off and he had a tidy little sum growing in the tin on his mantlepiece. Some, mostly members of his own family, scoffed at Bagsy's powers. The brothers were dubious as to his motivations and the curious reason as to why his powers had only appeared now, when Alannah had got wind of their purported existence.

Bagsy expanded his collection of curing accoutrements. Holy oil was ordered in from Medjugorje, a hexagon St Benedict bottle with blessed water arrived from Lourdes, and a vast array of different coloured candles from Amazon. He learned some more prayers and looked up a few more spells, blending Catholicism with internet witchcraft to create his own unique blend of spiritual awakening. A fella from Tullow with a gammy leg walked for the first time in a decade without a limp. A couple from Tinryland brought their daughter, a poor craythur who'd been mute from birth. Naer a word spoken and her five years old – didn't she only utter *Mammy* on the drive home?

Each success contributed to the gradual erosion of the hard shell of scepticism that ordinarily protected Bagsy from the harsh disappointments of life that those more optimistic were forced to reckon with. It was becoming increasingly difficult to deny that a lot of folks were living greatly improved lives following a visit to Bagsy Mahoney.

'Should we set up an Instagram for you, Darren?' Alannah asked, in her endless quest to capitalise on her boyfriend's new-found talents. She'd taken to calling him by his Christian name on the basis that it sounded more serious, carried more weight, and distinguished him from his feckless brothers.

'You could make it in the US, I bet,' she continued, wistfully. 'We could go to LA.'

But Bagsy knew that Instagram, LA, or any of that stuff wasn't his "brand", as they said. Rural, remote; mystical backwoods – this was his stock in trade and what had them coming. And didn't he hate the heat anyway.

By the time he was asked to perform the exorcism, Bagsy had all but bought into the idea that he really did have it, the cure, the gift, the power to change lives. The couple of grand in the tin on the mantelpiece went a long way in convincing him.

The exorcism, it had been decided, would be performed in the back shed of the house where Bagsy stored the turf for winter. That way, Alannah reasoned, there was less chance of the evil spirit, or whatever it was, from being let loose in his home. Bagsy pushed down the deep sense of unease that was rising from his core and the small voice in his head told him he should maybe sit this one out. Wasn't he helping the fella? Still, he knew he had to be careful, recalling an incident in primary school when a group of lads, his brother Jimmy among them, had been playing with a Ouija board and it spelled out that one of them would be dead within the year. Although the prophecy had been a bit off, timing wise, didn't people nod their heads knowingly when, a few years later, the car Philly Hoolihan had stolen had careered into a ditch at 180 kilometres per hour, killing him instantly?

Jimmy was quick to warn him against the planned exorcism, as were the other brothers.

They were jealous, he thought, just like his mother had always said.

'Now lad, do you really want to be messing around with this stuff? It's quare dangerous to get mixed up with Lucifer himself,' Paul said. 'And in my feckin' house too.'

'It's not *in* the house, I told you that,' he'd responded.

'He's right, son,' the Bag had added. 'Sure, even the priests stay away from this stuff.'

His father had made a sudden re-entrance to his life around the time that the brothers got wind of his improved financial situation. He took great pride in being the man responsible for this gift his son possessed, like his inability to keep his dick in his trousers had been some honourable and noble sacrifice.

'You're all overreacting,' he said, draining his pint and leaving for home, hoping that he was right.

Bagsy was nervous as they set up, clearing years of dirt and debris from the turf shed and replacing them instead with the cream and gold candles that he'd chosen for the ritual. Incense was burned. In preparation, he'd watched that old film, *Stigmata*, where Gabriel Byrne did an exorcism on this hot blonde wan, but it scared the bejaysus out of him and the blonde appeared to die at the end of it. Not good. Alannah had done some research too. Mrs Maguire, wife of Danny, she discovered, had inherited a decent whack from her father the year before and was a generous woman to those who helped her out. He'd be lying if he said this wasn't at the forefront of his mind when a shivering and growling Danny arrived for the ritual.

Once handsome, the march to middle age had claimed both Danny Maguire's natural good looks and any interest he had in keeping them. His large stomach strained at the buttons of his checked shirt, and he wore the drooping, sagging jowls of a life lived in a perpetual grind. But it was his eyes that unnerved Bagsy, those cold, unflickering windows into the darkness.

Leading him inside, Bagsy asked him to kneel at a kind of makeshift altar which he'd constructed from the old toolboxes and pieces of wood in the corner. Then he proceeded to tie ropes around the man's wrists with the other end tied to the barn doors – Danny easily weighed 250 pounds and he wasn't risking him or whatever it was inside of him physically attacking him. Next, he lit candles. The incense had been burning for hours and the scent of frankincense and myrrh permeated the charged atmosphere. As Bagsy began to pray, he sprinkled Danny with holy water, causing the man to react, pulling at the ropes and muttering incoherently. Emboldened by the reaction, Bagsy began to freestyle,

beseeching the spirit to leave Danny alone and to free the
man of his evil spirit. The louder he prayed, the more irate
Danny became. His eyes blackened and a tirade of incoher-
ent bile poured from his mouth.

Bagsy paced the floor, yelling for the beast to exit the
soul and to return to hell. An energy grew inside of him, and
he felt it – a raw power, an unshakeable spirituality, a con-
nection to a higher being. Bagsy knew with certainty that
he had the cure, that he was blessed with a gift and that it
was his duty in life to save people from evil and sickness
and all that was wrong with the world. The voice inside of
him let out a roar and in a fit of spiritual exuberance, he
threw the entire bottle of Medjugorje water over Danny's
head, causing the man to suddenly freeze in silence before
shuddering and bursting into tears. The ecstatic electric energy that had howled through the barn had been doused,
like a popped balloon. The monster had been exorcised and
Bagsy had never felt more vital, more alive, than he did in
that moment.

It was a couple of weeks later when he was in Tully's, enjoying a Friday night pint after work and waiting to meet
the brothers. Brendan had called to say there was somebody who he wanted to introduce him to. Another poor soul
in need of help, perhaps, for surely now, even the brothers
would struggle to refute the existence of his healing powers.
Since the business with Danny Maguire, Bagsy, shocked to
the core by the strength of his own powers, had been laying

low at home and conducting research into how he might expand his practice. Triona Maguire had, just as Alannah predicted, dropped in an envelope of cash – more cash than he'd ever seen – a day after the exorcism. Bagsy was contemplating quitting the factory now. Going full time with the spirituality. He was a bit like a priest but without the celibacy and without having to listen to auld ones tell you their sins. It wasn't right to profit from other people's misfortune, he knew that, but it was hard to find the time or the headspace to help people when he was spending fifty hours a week digging out ribs by hand with a hook.

'Well, there he is now, Jesus Christ himself,' Brendan said, walking into the pub, his voice weighty with sarcasm. 'Will you be walking over water?'

Brendan was the oldest and the biggest prick of the lot of them.

'Fuck off with that now.'

'Does he not know?' Jimmy asked.

'Know what?'

'Haven't told him yet,' Paul sniggered.

'Sure we'll introduce him shortly. He'll be here soon.'

'Who will?' Bagsy asked.

At that moment, as though in response to his very question, into the pub walked a man, maybe two or three years older than himself. There was something familiar about him, though Bagsy was confident he had never met the man before.

'This is Dylan. From up in Dublin, isn't that right?' Brendan said, the shadow of a smirk dancing in the corners of his mouth.

Dylan nodded and his eyes rested on Bagsy. He saw it then. The Mahoney eyes, peering out at him, as familiar as any of his brothers.

'Dylan just tracked down his long-lost father, didn't yeh? Brendan paused and fixed his eyes on Bagsy. 'And you'll never guess who his dear old Da is?'

'None other than The Bag himself,' Paul answered without missing a beat. 'Born just a year before myself, he was.'

Bagsy felt as though the oxygen was being slowly sucked from the air and reached out his arm and grabbed the bar to steady himself. That their father acted like he'd been single-handedly chosen to save the human race from extinction was not something that had escaped Bagsy's attention, and while he'd always acknowledged there was a fair chance there was another brother or even a sister out there, what hadn't occurred to him, was how it might upset the chronology of the family. Maths had never been his strong point but Bagsy could see where this was going.

'Of course, you know what this means,' Paul said to him, a sly grin on his face. 'If Dylan here was born a year before me, it's not you who is the seventh son.'

'Ssshh,' Bagsy whispered, conscious that Sheila of the shingles was sitting just inches away in the snug next to the bar. 'Keep your voice down.'

'It's me,' Paul continued.

'But... the worm...' was all Bagsy managed to stutter out.

'Ah sure, who's to say it wasn't already dead. Fr O'Toole could have been telling Ma what she wanted to hear.'

'I've helped people, Paul. That poor Maguire fella – I drove the devil himself from his soul.'

As he said the words, words he had been so confident in just minutes before, they sounded hollow and empty and well, completely ridiculous.

'Sure he was always a mad bastard. Probably a flashback from the mushrooms,' Dermot scoffed.

Sheila, earwigging next to them, stood and turned to him.

'I knew you were a charlatan, a bloody snake oil salesman,' she snapped, pulling up her arm to reveal red flaking, scaly skin. 'Didn't it come back just this week? And now I hear you don't have the cure at all?' she said with an expression that would turn milk.

Bagsy raised his hands in a show of defence.

'I sold you nothing, Sheila. I never charged you.'

She had dropped in a gift of one hundred euro, mind. And when this got out, there'd be other people looking for money from him, and all. Around him, people tutted and rolled their eyes and the brothers just laughed and laughed, even Dylan, settling right in with the Bagsies.

Later that night, stewing in whiskey and self-pity, Bagsy clutched his tin of money and thought back over the events of the previous six months. Sheila's shingles had cleared up – that they'd come back couldn't be attributed to him. He remembered the mute child who spoke for the first time, the farmer from Laois whose ringworm vanished and, whatever excuses and reasons that his brothers might offer, driving the devil from the soul of Danny Maguire. He remembered the feeling of power and purpose and people relying on him for more than skinning carcasses in sub-zero temperatures. Bagsy didn't care how many brothers he had or how hard they laughed at him; he wasn't letting that go. His life of gristle and bone was over – he was a healer, and the world needed his help.

Elin Olausson

Them

While Ella scrubbed the algae from China's feet she was humming, their usual morning ritual. Tooth stood by her side, watching, scratching his hair.

'When's it my turn?'

The children were always asking questions but she was used to it, didn't mind. 'As soon as your sister is nice and clean. You could use the comb while you wait.'

He shrugged and plopped down on the floor, pulling his knees up. Stubby boy-fingers picked at the brownish smears on his soles and she wanted to tell him to stop, but he was getting his wash soon anyway. No need to get into a fight.

'There, that's better.' She pulled her hands out of the pail and told China to put on her slippers, the crocheted ones that Sweet had made. China slunk away and Tooth took her place, splashing around with his dirty feet.

'Why do we have to be clean?' he asked while she was crouching down, sticking her hands back into the muddy water.

'Because we are people and not beasts,' Ella told him like Mother had once told her.

'Oh.' Tooth splashed around some more, until she towelled his little feet and he got into his slippers and ran off. Ella grabbed the pail and took it outside, throwing the contents over the mayweeds. The air was chilly, the mist thick as milk.

'Stay indoors now, hear?' she called to the children, but there was no reply, as if they had slipped into that liquid white nothingness and left her behind. Ella rushed back into the house, chest strained as she dropped the pail on the floor and hurried into the kitchen. They couldn't have gone. They wouldn't.

'Children?' she called, and in the same moment she saw them, lounging in front of the fire. China leaned her head on Tooth's shoulder and they were talking together in that secret language only they could understand. Ella softened, sank down on the chair and closed her eyes. For a moment she was going to enjoy the crackling fire, the warmth, the sound of their tiny voices. The bells would tell her if something bad happened. Sweet had constructed the system and he was good with things like that, there wasn't a spot he hadn't wired, hadn't marked on his map. The map was still here, hidden away in the desk drawer, even if Sweet wasn't. Sometimes she took it out and traced the island edges with her thumb. They made a zigzag pattern, crags and rocky shores, bushes sprouting here and there. She had explored the island as a child, stumbling along the waterline, Mother's screams hounding her. It was long ago and she knew better now, knew why Sweet had put up the wires. Why the mist came.

After supper, she took a seat in between the children and opened the book. Tooth and China loved being read to, always snuggled up close to her and asked her to repeat words or entire pages.

'Is the big world like this?' Tooth said, pointing at the picture, the buildings rising towards the sky. 'Are the people out there giants?'

'No, silly.' China sighed, arranging her shift over her stick legs. 'The houses are tall because many people live in them.'

Ella nodded, careful not to praise China for her knowledge. Tooth's jealousy was rare but unpleasant, and best avoided. 'The big world is much more than this,' she said, as the City unfolded in her brain. The City, and the oily tang that came with it.

'How big is it then?' Tooth asked, clinging to her arm, close enough that she could hear him wheeze. 'The world, does it go on forever and ever? Are there lots of people there?'

Ella looked into the fire, the way it danced. 'No,' she said, recalling Mother's words. 'Not anymore.'

After the children had been tucked in bed she stayed up, preparing a dough for the next morning, reheating some tea. The nights, they were the low point. She covered the windows, put up the big boards Sweet had constructed using driftwood and rope. Tomorrow she would remove them, but only when the sun was shining through.

She turned her head to watch the children, the room quiet around her, and a familiar dread filled her as she rushed over, lifting the blanket to make sure they hadn't gone. China stirred, but Tooth's face was peaceful and he seemed lost in dreams.

'You stay here,' she whispered, thinking about the City and the pantry that was almost empty. 'I'll keep you safe.'

She decided to head out two days later, when the weather was warm and a fire wasn't needed except for tea. They were getting older, they could handle basic tasks, but she still didn't like the thought of them striking fire or chopping wood.

'I'll be back before you know it,' she told them, kissing grimy little foreheads, stroking coarse white hair. 'And I promise I'll bring back a gift for you.'

'Is it fruit?' asked Tooth, who had memorised plenty of words from the book. 'Is it candy?'

'I don't know yet what it is,' she said, throwing the bag over one shoulder and glancing into the cottage. 'Now go back inside and be good while I'm away. You know what to do at nightfall, don't you?'

'Don't look outside,' they chanted. 'Bar the door. Put the boards up. Sleep.'

'That's right.' She lifted her hand in a wave and went down the path, heels drumming against rocks, flies whirring in the air. Tooth and China would be fine, because they had been every other time, but still she felt awful leaving them alone. It had been easier when Mother was around, and Sweet too, though he wasn't easy to handle.

Your brother is as stubborn as a mule, Mother had said, and Ella had laughed although she had no idea what a mule was. There weren't any mules in the book, but perhaps she had passed by one in the City without knowing. A glaring, willful thing that wouldn't budge.

The boat was where she had left it, in that dead spot behind the buckthorn, where nothing grew. Dragging it across the shore was heavy work, but she used it so little and storms rattled the island at times, when Sea was angry or spiteful or bored. Today she was at peace, though, a pale blue that stretched out towards the big world. Towards the mist. As Ella pushed the boat into the water, it played at the edge of her vision, strands of milk, a nothingness with claws.

'I see you,' she muttered, thinking about Tooth and China in the cottage. 'We both know where we have each other.'

The oars were heavy; as she lifted them, two little marks on the right one caught her eye. Something skulked through her mind, a furry thing, but creatures like that lived only in the City and not here. Sweat dampened her back and she forced the fear away, it was nothing, posed no threat. All she needed to do was go across the water, pick up supplies, and head back. The children would be fine while she was gone.

The mist watched as she rowed, snickering as she rubbed her shoulder or groaned from exhaustion. It didn't come any closer, but it didn't vanish either.

The City sneaked up on her like always. It was only after she spotted the skeletal buildings that towered over the port that she became aware of the smell, that nauseating blend of rot and toxic waste. It reminded her to tie the neckerchief over her nose and mouth, a precaution she took every visit, even as Sweet had said it was futile. The City was quiet, except for the lapping of waves and a distant creak that might be a building slowly collapsing on itself. Perhaps years from now, when the children went into the City on their own, all the tall scrapers would be in ruins.

Ella secured the boat in the spot by the pier, below the ladder that was rusty but still climbable. After stowing the oars away and grabbing her backpack she ascended, wincing as the ladder's corroding metal touched her skin. Ideally, she would have worn gloves, but Mother's old pair had been lost somewhere and she hadn't found any new ones on her last trip.

The pier was a sickly arm stretching into the water and she hurried across, skipping past the gaps in the concrete. One day she would come here and it would be torn apart, but that day wasn't now and she had to focus. Watch the ground in front of her for puddles and slippery weeds, scan the docks for movement. Think as little as possible about the scrapers and their many windows, because if you did it could make you mad. Just look what had happened to Sweet.

As soon as she reached the quayside, the smell grew into a putrid stench, and she pressed the neckerchief to her face. The smell was unpleasant but familiar, no cause for alarm. Any other scents, that was what Mother had taught them to be wary of. Smoke and food, fresh cadavers. Rumbling sounds in the distance, and any new marks or traces that seemed human-made.

But there are no humans left, she and Sweet had said, round-eyed, in front of the fire a lifetime ago. Mother had shook her head and said, *Until I've searched every single corner of that place, I can't say for sure.*

After examining the docks and finding the ruins as desolate as expected, Ella slipped into the usual alley. Sweet had cleaned it up before he left, had spent days dragging away scraps of metal and sweeping glass shards into the gutter. There had been a body, too – Ella had never seen it, but Sweet had told her what it looked like, bright white teeth in a grinning mouth, a few blonde hairs glued to the scalp.

I pushed her into the water so she wouldn't be out in the open like that with her bosom showing.

Pattering through the alley, Ella wondered where Sweet had found the woman, and what it was that had killed her. Had she been running towards the docks, or had she gone the other way? The thought occupied her mind as she went into the pharmacy, the one that marked the end of the alley and the beginning of Rain Street. Mother had said that it wasn't really called Rain Street, but once in her youth she'd been out with a boy she liked, and they'd walked down that street when a shower of rain had hit them, ruining her hair and her prettiest dress. After that, she and her friends started referring to it as Rain Street, and the name had stuck.

Rummaging through the pharmacy drawers, blocking out the smell of chemicals and decaying rodents, Ella remembered hearing that story as a child, struggling to comprehend it.

But you can't live in the City, she'd said, and Mother had smiled and told her, *Once upon a time you could.*

She left the pharmacy with three bottles of painkillers, gauze, and iodine. The drawers were almost empty now, and she couldn't remember how much had been left after her last visit. Maybe she should search for another pharmacy, farther away from the docks, but the idea sickened her. The longer she stayed in this place, the more dangerous it became.

The toy store smelled of mould and plastic, and the dollies stared at her as she grabbed a yo-yo and a rubber ball. Dust stuck to her hands and she wiped them on her thighs as she sneaked back into the street. Coming back home without gifts was unthinkable.

Clothes were next on the list, and food last. She'd look for a pair of gloves, stuff her backpack with canned beans, and head back. If she hurried, she might make it before nightfall.

She was outside the department store when she heard it. The whining. Reaching for her knife, she held her breath, gazing into the darkness behind the revolving doors. A big rat, or a feral dog? She'd faced both before but wasn't keen to relive the experience. Judging by the sound it was wounded, though, and probably not much of a threat. And she wanted those gloves.

The doors creaked as she pushed them. The air was heavy with dust and she coughed, pressing one hand to her face.

'Just passing through, passing through, passing through...' The chanting hit her as she stumbled into the big hallway, and she stepped back, shoulder bumping against the doorframe.

'Please help me. I won't stay here, I promise to God. I'm only a traveller,' the voice rambled, a male voice that was smoother than Sweet's and perhaps younger, too. 'I didn't know, I... I just wanted to take a look in here and then I fell and hurt my leg. I'm no danger to you, I swear. My name's Theodore. What's yours?'

It unnerved her that he seemed to be able to see her, when she had no idea what he looked like. Reluctantly, she removed the flashlight from her front pocket and aimed it into the darkness. The beam fell on litter and broken tiles, rusty cans, and an unmoving bundle in the corner. Then, she realised that the bundle was a body, with a pair of stretched-out legs. One was twisted, blood dripping from the foot and ankle. The light snaked over a baggy jacket, a knitted scarf, and a shock of black hair. In between that hair a face, gaunt and stubbly and strangely clean.

'Don't hurt me.' He put his hands up, stared with slanted eyes. 'Just stay calm. Won't you tell me your name?'

Her eyes were drawn back to his wound, the bloodied concrete floor. 'It's Ella.'

'Ella? I like that, that's a good name. Don't think I've heard it before. Hey, Ella, do you know if...' He groaned, body contorting. 'I'm sorry, I know you don't trust me. I wouldn't trust myself either. It's just, my foot hurts like hell and I don't know what to do about it.'

Ella had seen her share of injuries, it was part of the island life, skin tearing and mending. Theodore would need to clean and dress that wound before it got infected, or he'd be sorry. Bad things could happen quickly, in the blink of an eye.

He gasped with parted lips and fluttering lashes, and she took a step closer.

'Where did you come from?'

'Oh, I... I'm from the North. We've only heard rumours about this place, so we wanted to investigate. Check for survivors, that's all.'

'We?' she asked, thinking about her knife and the shadows listening in.

'Don't worry, it's just me here. I went out on my own, and boy, do I regret it. Look, um, is there any chance at all you could help me? I don't think I can get out of here by myself.'

The light beam trailed over him again, those lean legs, the blood on the concrete spreading. Ella's insides burned with the knowledge of the gauze and iodine in her bag, the pills that could ease his pain.

'You can't follow me,' she said as she moved over, knife held tight. 'I don't know who you are.'

'I'm Theodore. I told you.' He groaned as she pulled at his trouser leg to expose the wound. The twin gashes made no sense until she saw the loose board beside him, nails sticking out. He must have tripped over it at the wrong angle.

'A name tells me nothing.' She removed the backpack and brought out the iodine, hoping he wouldn't ask. The pharmacy was hers. 'What is it like where you come from? How many people are there?'

Theodore drew shallow breaths as she cleaned the wound. 'It's... It's an old settlement. Used to be a farm. Sala's the nearest town, though it's barely populated anymore. Unless you count the ghosts.'

Ella pushed his sock out of the way and grabbed the gauze. 'There are no ghosts.'

'How do you know? Have you looked for yourself, then? Travelled the world?' He smirked, and she wrapped his ankle snugly to wipe the smile off his face.

'What world? I can't go anywhere. There's the mist.' *And the children.*

'Yeah, I noticed. Is it always foggy here?'

Ella thought about Sweet and his wires, his shiny eyes. 'Always. Especially at night.'

'Strange. I've never seen anything like it.'

She finished the bandage and took a step back, putting her things back in the bag. All this talk about the big world, she didn't like it. Still his words were like hooks, luring her in.

'Care to help me stand?' he asked, lifting his hand. 'Please?'

In her head Tooth and China called, but their voices were small and Theodore was smiling again. She reached out, allowing him to lean on her. Once he stood, he was just a few inches taller and it made her less afraid. He was wounded, weak, and she had Mother's old knife to protect her.

'So, how many live here?' he asked as she led the way into the dark, towards the supermarket. 'I couldn't see a single trace on my way in.'

'The City is empty,' she said, scanning the floor for glass or dead animals. 'The mist took everyone, made them mad.'

'I thought it was that thing with the power plant,' Theodore said. 'Then the tsunami. That's what my grandmother says, anyway.'

Ella wondered what a tsunami was but didn't want to ask. 'No, that's not what happened. The mist came and then it never left. It's hungry and eats people's minds.'

Theodore laughed. 'Okay.'

'Like my brother when he–' She stopped herself, didn't want to talk about Sweet. 'Here, this is the supermarket. We can find food.'

They went inside the wide, low-ceilinged space, light beam bouncing ahead. Some shelves had collapsed, others were brimming with rotting food or packaging torn by rodent teeth. The canned supplies were in the fourth aisle, she knew it well, had been here many times. Ever since Mother left, it had been her duty.

'What do you mean, *mad*?' Theodore asked as she stuffed heavy cans into the backpack, beans and tomatoes, chicken noodle soup. 'In what way?'

'Well, they... They just broke down. There was something about the mist that made them hurt other people. Or hurt themselves.'

'Like a disease. A sickness of the mind.'

'Maybe.'

They went back towards the mall's entrance, Ella staggering from carrying the backpack and supporting Theodore. Through the revolving doors she saw the fading light outside, the first licks of the mist rolling by.

'How about you?' he asked, quieter than before. 'How come you live here, if what you said is true?'

She turned to look at him, those eyes, the gold in them. 'I don't live in the City. Mother found an island for us, where it's safe. I only come here now and then for supplies.'

Theodore frowned and she heard Mother's words in her head, cold and barbed. *The island is only safe as long as no one else knows about it.*

'Do you live alone?'

Tooth and China stared up at her, smooth faces, beady eyes. 'There's the... No, I'm alone.'

'The what?' He smelled of sweat and dirt, but she was used to it. 'You have a husband? Kids?'

She stared into the mist-trails on the other side of the door. 'Children. Two of them.'

'Two, wow. I haven't seen any kids in forever. How old are they?'

Ella's skin burned and she wondered how many questions he had left; if they would ever end. 'I don't really know. Old enough to be left alone for a few days.'

'You ever bring them here?'

'No!' She realised too late that she'd shouted. 'I go by myself. It's not safe.'

'There's no safe place in this world,' he said, his voice ageing as he spoke. Turning grey. 'Just temporary shelters. Who knows what things will be like at the farm when I get back? One crack, that's all it takes. One rift in the wall.'

The word *shelter* made something click, brushed the mist away. 'There's a place close by, we use it sometimes. When we need to stay overnight.' She started walking, moving towards the doors, but he stopped her.

'I thought you said the children never come here.'

'I meant my mother, my brother.' *Sweet and his wires, his broken grin.* 'Mother was the one who brought us here, showed us where to scavenge. And where to hide.'

'But she's gone now?' Theodore asked, and she nodded.

'Everything's gone,' she said.

The apartment was three stories up, white-walled and cold, but it was free of corpses and the windows had been barred, presumably by the person who once lived there. Ella hated going up the stairs, passing all those doors that might open at any moment, revealing a dweller who'd been lurking inside, waiting for the sound of footsteps. Once they had reached the apartment she locked the door, which lessened her paranoia just a little. Someone could force the door open if they really tried, but at least she'd get a warning first.

After helping Theodore into the bedroom, she opened a can and poured half of the chicken soup into her mouth before handing Theodore the rest.

'It's good,' he said, and she remembered another night in this room, Mother eating from a can and sobbing. *I want proper food. I want green apples and pizza.*

'How is your foot?'

'Not great, but it'll be healed up soon. I'm not worried.'

Did anyone miss him – a girl on that farm, a dark-eyed stranger? Ella didn't want to know. She took the emptied can from him and unzipped her jacket, and when she grabbed his hand it was warm and alive. If he was taken aback he didn't show it, just made room for her, covered them both with the blanket. And the night smiled.

They stayed cooped up the next day, and the day after that. Ella went out in the morning to find a walking stick for Theodore and get those gloves she'd forgotten about, and when she came back he was sleeping. A light shape in a filthy room, a brightness in the mist.

'I need to go back,' she said once he stirred, yawning, showing uneven teeth. 'To the children.'

'Can I come?' he asked, just like she'd known he would. His question tore at her, made the bedroom smaller.

'They're not used to people,' she said, picturing the draughty kitchen, their sticky feet.

'Are any of us?' Theodore smiled, caressed her hand, and in a lost world Mother walked down Rain Street arm in arm with a boy. The kind of thing that only happened in the past but maybe, just this once, she could have a Rain Street of her own.

They walked down to the docks after emptying another lukewarm can. The end of the stick drummed against the pavement and Ella wondered if anyone could hear it, if there were heads and fingers stirring. In a city where Theodore existed, others could exist as well.

'I've never been in a boat,' he said as they climbed down the ladder, Ella grateful for her gloves. 'I've only seen them in pictures.'

What sort of pictures? she wanted to ask but didn't, because one question easily turned into another, like when Tooth begged her for stories. Once Theodore was settled, bag between his knees, she took the oars and started rowing. The scrapers watched her leave, silent, tall as gods.

'I think the world will be whole again,' he said when they were out on the water, Sea stretching out below. 'Maybe not like it was, but close.'

'Mother said the world was never whole.' Ella lifted the oars, recalling the lines around Mother's eyes. Her mist-white hair.

'I don't mind,' he said, smiling, leaning to the side. Watching his blurry reflection. 'As long as I can find my own little corner to live in.'

She wondered what he would think about her island. The rocks and wires.

'I see it,' Theodore said a while later, craning his neck. 'Will the children notice we're coming, will they come out to greet us?'

His excitement rubbed off on her, making her row faster. 'They know to be wary of strangers.'

'Even if the stranger is in their mother's company?' He grinned, patted her thigh, and she forced her facial muscles not to twitch at the sound of that word.

'We'll see,' she said, head filling with tasks to handle: row ashore, secure the boat, put the backpack on. Tell Theodore about the wires so he wouldn't trigger the alarm.

After reaching the island, she stood for a moment and inhaled the air, salt and tar. Theodore felt the cliff, the buckthorn twigs.

'It smells different. I can't say exactly what it is, but there's something unusual here.' He grinned, and although she knew where they'd met it was hard to believe that he was that dirty, injured stranger she'd found in the mall. The harder she thought about it, the more it seemed as if the island had brought him to life, made him real.

'Can I meet the children now?' he asked, fidgeting with a buckthorn leaf, tearing it in two. Ella thought about Tooth and China behind the locked door, whispering to each other in their made-up language.

'I don't want to scare them.'

He frowned. 'They'll want to see their mother. You've been gone for days.'

'I'm not their mother,' she said, feeling faint. 'I'm just someone who lives with them.'

Theodore shook his head, letting the torn leaf slip from his hand. 'Are there any children here at all?'

'Yes!' She stared at him, pulse quickening. 'They're in the cottage, they're called Tooth and China, and they're mine.'

'Then let's go and meet them.' Theodore started walking through the undergrowth, his stick slamming against the rocks. She saw the wires shiver and ached to tell him about the bells, how they made the cottage cry, but she couldn't. Stumbling after him she tried to come up with an excuse, a reason for him not to open that door.

It's mine. It's my little corner.

When he reached the yard, Theodore stopped and sniffed the air. 'The smell is different up here. When I was lying on that mall floor, this is what it smelled like.'

'You wanted to see the cottage,' she said, stomach twisting. 'Here it is.'

'I wanted to see the children.' The walking stick hit the ground again and he went straight up to the door, trying the handle. Turned back to frown at her when the door opened. 'No lock?'

Ella didn't say anything. It was too late.

When she entered the cottage he stood by the hearth, towering over the children. They were in front of the hearth where she had left them, and she heard them tittering in their little voices.

'What is this?' Theodore grabbed China's arm and lifted her. 'What have you done?' He turned the child around, then dropped her with a yelp.

'Don't treat her like that!' Ella rushed forwards, gathered them in her arms. Stroked their mist-white hair. 'I won't let you hurt them.'

Theodore stared at her. He had no smiles left. 'Who were they?' He put his hand over his mouth. 'The people you... Who were they?'

Ella both did and didn't understand the question. He didn't know how lonely it could get when the mist rolled in, when it swallowed everything. He didn't know what it was like to live with a brother who muttered about rotting women, or a mother who did nothing but cry.

He didn't know that you needed someone, or you'd go mad.

'It's revolting,' he said, taking a step back. 'It's sick.'

Ella caressed Tooth's bony cheek and whispered that the man wasn't angry at them and that he would leave soon, so there was nothing to be scared about.

'You're crazy,' Theodore hissed and limped out of the cottage. She went over to the door and watched him go, wondering if he was scared, if he thought he'd die and become another island child. After a few minutes the bells started ringing, one after the other, as he tripped the wires. Through the trees and bushes she saw him struggle with the boat rope, then throw himself in the water. As if something was chasing him, hunting him down. Across the water the mist drifted closer, as if it had waited, watched from afar. Ella pitied Theodore, she would have liked for him to stay, but Sea was always hungry and he was too delicious for her to spare.

In Ella's arms Tooth stirred, pressed against her. 'Who was that man?' he asked.

'Yes, who was he?' China said, curling up against Ella's chest.

'It doesn't matter anymore. Now, let's see what I brought you from the City. After that I'll tell you a story.'

Shalini Srinivasan

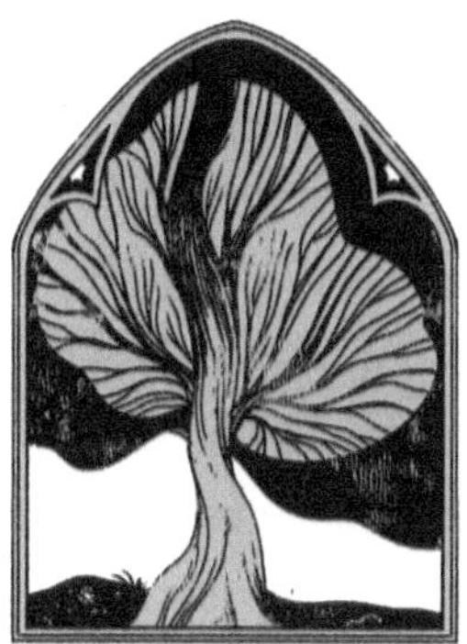

What's Empty in the House of Smoke?

An Ethnographic Enquiry into its Population, Diversity, and History

by Impatiens Balsamina (var. loqui)

Keywords: Houses, smoke, plantae, fungi, diversity

Introduction

From the human point of view, the House of Smoke is flawless. It is welcoming of visitors from far away. Unlike some other houses, it is open to all: caste, class, religion, gender, region, sexuality, and race are meaningless here. Eating habits are no barrier, since no one eats in the House anyway. No one in the House of Smoke will demand a passport, a seal, a number, a proof of citizenship, identity or existence. "If you are there, then you are a guest of the House," notes the traveller-poet Ammani in a copper plate inscription dated 678 AD. "The only requirement is that you must – while you visit – shrug off your body and take on the air. Be smoke." (See Mahadevan 2007 for more details.)

I attempted to experience this for myself.

The doors of the House open every morning at dawn, revealing a glass-roofed antechamber. The doorwoman was most courteous. She guided me through the process of disembodiment – a drink, a syringe, a bed of ice for the guest, the weaving of song and loom. The doorwoman's voice is frail these days; her notes may waver, her hands may tremble. There is nothing to worry about: she sings true and the loom dips and rises to her will.

Then, Ammani states, comes "the waning, the weightless calm of rising out of your body, into smoke."

But the House was meant for human physiology, human chemistry. I remained full, earthbound.

The House Guide tapestry that hangs upon the wall of the antechamber says:

> The doorwoman will cool your body and stack it in the underground ice chambers, so it will remain unaged through your visit. Twice a year, great ice blocks are cut from Himalayan glaciers, and brought down the river in barges pulled by blind dolphins. The ice, it is said, will cool your body, now freed from your incessant presence, of all its sorrows and ailments.
>
> Do not fear – your body will not be mixed up with others. The House has a many-layered and strict policy to ensure the intactness and returnability of

bodies. The doorwoman will weave the identifying markers of your body into a coarse scarf made of the wool of the Deccani goat, known for its stubbornness and resistance to being wiped out. The scarf will be wrapped around the ankles of the body, keeping it immovable until your return. You will receive a bracelet of the finest hair from the body (plucked from the tender skin inside your wrists, perhaps, where it is best suited to flying) marking you as each other's.

The doorwoman is an excellent judge of character. She will select from among the finest incenses and perfumes and herbs and pick the smoke-garb that will waft each guest into the inner chambers of the House of Smoke. (Unknown Author)

The tapestry is largely accurate in its description of the disembodiment process. The centrality of the doorwoman's role will be explored later in this essay, and my interviews with and observations of her are crucial to this paper's argument. The tapestry's testimony must be supplemented with a more critical reading. *Caravan Creepers: A Pilgrim's Guide to the Houses of the World* offers a vegetal view from the early twenty-first century that is largely corroborated by my own research:

From the botanical point of view, the House of Smoke is sparsely populated. Only the lichens are permitted regular entry, trapped within ice blocks that will, eventually, melt, and send them out into the world in the tiniest and most glacial of trickles.

Other than the lichens, the stone walls of the House hold only the botanical dead – wood, incense, perfume, soot.

> It is not a House designed for or by the denizens of the kingdoms plantae, algae, fungi. (Wallerina, 2004, pp. 34)

Unlike, for instance, the Houses of Inching and of Deeps, the House of Smoke was, I argue, built by humans, for their narrow, animalian, sole, *homo sapiens* use. This paper will show that the House, unusually for one so long-lived, failed to consider one of the vital properties of the plantly (and the algal and the fungal) – the ability to lie dormant for millennia before rising up again.

Section I. Interviews and notes from my first fieldwork sessions, May–June 2034. This section will discuss the state of the House in 2034, depicting conditions in the house before the Opening began.

1. May 4th, 2034. Interview with Savithribaayi, Doorwoman (now retired), House of Smoke.

"I wore my indigo block-printed saree on my first day to work. And at least once a week after that. Sometimes, I regretted the loss of corporeality among the other dwellers in the house. Clothing was my lonely interest.

"The loom is older than the House of Smoke. Few things were, but carved into the loom's stand are the jagged letters of a language so old no one even remembers it. This too is a body, left behind in the quiet stasis of the house. And its spirit is not smoke, to wait and linger in the House for a delayed return – it is simply, entirely, gone.

"When thoughts of agedness and looms occur in my mind, I tug on the heavy iron ring that holds the trapdoor

closed. Then I slide the trapdoor open and lower my body – increasingly achy and disobedient – through the opening and climb down the rungs to the body-chambers below."

2. Interview with the smoke of 'Abd Al-samad Shirazi, resident since **1589** (approx.). The interviewee was briefly corporealized for the interview.

"What is the House of Smoke, you ask? That's a hard question, easier shown than said."[1]

"In words, then: it is upon the great river and under it; there are tinkly-leaved trees set around its compound walls that stir the air; the walls are made of the finest pink marble, polished and inlaid with delicate shards of amethyst and lapis laid to look like the evening sky glittering upon the river's surface; the sun beats hot upon the tallest domes in summer and the river evaporates and everyone in the House shimmers; the watermelons that grow every summer in the drying riverbed next to the House are said to be the sweetest in Asia."

3. Ethnographer's reflections

Below the House, it was always cool, damp, a reminder that the river was their neighbour, its water seeping into everything. The bodies – abandoned, slack and unaware – lay in the neat rows the doorwoman had planned. Each was placed in a sort of ice-sandwich, ice below, ice above, a sliver of blue-tinted skin peering out between.

---

1. **Ethnographer's note:** The interviewee, a miniaturist, tried to draw the House on my notes, but his fingers cramped from disuse.

The doorwoman planned her paths among the bodies like she planned the arrangements of threads in a loom. She liked to sort them, mentally, by various things – height, hair style, footwear, the colours of their skins, the arch of their foreheads. She wove over and around the bodies with precision.

Alone among the denizens of the house, the doorwoman craved touch. She ran her fingers on the loom above, always stroking, touching, arranging. Below, she slid her hands through hair, coarse, greasy, silken, strawish. She ran her fingertips over the clothes – khadi, satin, silk, muslin, the sudden solid chill of a button of wood or ivory or brass. Her palms were cupped below noses to catch the faintest gasp of air, moving in, moving out.

Their names were carved into the ice, and the doorwoman murmured them to the ice-shielded ears lest they feel utterly abandoned.

Sometimes, she murmured one other name, lest it too melt and trickle into the ground unused, never to be recovered. This was her own name.

It was here that the doorwoman, Savithribaayi, came to feel a real rapport with me. After I heard her name, I was careful to speak it; I wrote it indelibly. Such is the ethnographer's burden and privilege.

Section II. Interviews and notes from my second fieldwork sessions, April–May 2035. This section provides evidence, and establishes that though 2036 is the official year of Opening, the process was set in motion a little more than a year prior.

1. Ethnographer's reflections, April 8th, 2035.

After the sun sets in the House of Smoke, the coolth is swift. The river washes away the heat of the day, and the marble domes turn chill. The smoke people move lower then, mist gathering in the valleys and crooks of the house. They sway and lurk and pool together until the fire goes out and the last wisps escape into the skies.

A secret of the house: this is the time in which the unwary visitor might be lost forever. Some follow the smoke up up up until the House can no longer shelter them. In the river breezes, the smoke simply disperses.

Sometimes a thin bracelet of hair falls on the riverbanks.

On these days, the doorwoman must enter the chambers and search for a withered scarf among the toes. Then she must take the cloth back to the loom.

The loom will pull select threads out of the scarf – a scar right there upon a sun-darkened neck; a finger truncated at just this angle. A brief snatch of old words, a stick of incense. The scarf will be, softly, undone.

A crash of ice from below will confirm – the body between will have vaporised to join the person. A gentle passing, the doorwoman remarked to me – the one she would choose if there were anyone to undo her.

**2. Interview with the temporarily recorporealized
'Abd Al-samad Shirazi, resident since 1589 (approx.),
April 9th, 2035.**

"In the evenings, a great bonfire is lit in the house. The doorwoman – the only inhabitant whose body is above ground

and available for occupation – builds a pile of logs, bitter neem and sweet camphor. She strikes flint – unimaginable solidity! unparalleled friction! – and throws the spark into the firepit. The inhabitants gather and sway in sympathy as the flames catch and roar and throw a dark sooty smoke into the air so it may mingle and seep into their empty corners.

"Above, the round domes of the House shine in the fire-light like moons thronging the courtyard.

"This is one of the singular joys of the House of Smoke."

3. Interview with Savithribaayi, Doorwoman (now retired), House of Smoke, May 12th, 2035.

"Evenings are quiet. I have a little kerosene stove to make a meal and eat it.

"Smoke does not need food; neither do bodies halted in their tracks by cold. Doorwomen are, uniquely in the House of Smoke, subject to hunger. We are subject also to other bodyish, outish things – fevers and tempers, bladders, bowels, and – until recently – uteruses; the aches of old bone-breaks when the river creeps too close.

"At midnight, I close the iron gates and bolt the wooden door that kept the House from the world. I tie the keys into one end of my sari, and tuck it in at my waist.

"I sleep above ground. But lately, it's been getting so hot, I have started using the bodychamber. I sleep at one end, where I won't disturb the others. At first, I went when the vast flashes of heat struck my body.[2] Only the mountain ice could quench those flames.

––––––––––––––––––––

2. **Interviewer's note:** A later interview revealed that, contrary to my expectations, the doorwoman was still intermittently at the mercy of her inefficient, mammalian uterus.

"Don't tell my employers, but one or two minor disturbances are unavoidable. Last month, for example, a toenail caught my sari and ripped through.

"Naturally, I examined the body – a woman, tall, almost as tall as her ice block. Her toes had acquired a greenblack tinge from cold and neglect. Beneath the ice, the outlines of her face were exquisitely softened by dripmelt and frost, only the dark sockets of her eyes visible.

"I bent and slid her toes back in, securing them. Something flowed out and wrapped itself around my wrist. I froze! A hand?

"No, it was soft, wavy. Hair? I tugged and it slipped out. Not hair, a scarf. The scarf, in fact, the scarf that held within it the bond between person and body.

"The cloth was silken and airy, which was all wrong. Many things are said of the hair of the Deccani goat – its resilience, its warmth, its ineffable strengthening of all magics laid in its vicinity[3] – but it is coarse. This scarf, though. Not silk, nor muslin. It was lighter than both and flowing like a river.

"I could not remember when the woman had entered, when the scarf had been woven – before my time. This was not surprising – smokepeople had been known to stay long, enraptured and scattered. When they returned to their bodies and left the house, their peoples and nations were gone. Only last year, a man had tumbled gracelessly into his body, kicking his scarf off with a scream. He had wept to see the river outside. When he'd entered the house, he said, there was no river, only flat scrubby forest. He flung himself into the jaws of a crocodile, rather than attempt a journey home."

----

3. See Varalakshmi, 1998

4. Ethnographer's reflections, May 12th, 2035.

I ran a leaf over the scarf. Recognition. Instant and sure. A long dormant fungus was awaking. Spores were beginning to rise into the air. Was it my presence? The melting ice?

I held the scarf for another minute, root to spore. I lent a few grains of mud, rich and red.

"Beautiful," I murmured.

We dropped a discreet hypha or two into each other, as was only polite. The doorwoman did not perceive it.

As a botanical graveyard, cenotaph, mausoleum, the House of Smoke was beginning to fail. Much ice had melted over the centuries. My transgression was small: many spores were dispersing from wet scarves and bodies, floating in the humid riverine air. I could feel the sparks as they caught, fed, grew.

Some parts of the house did, after all, receive sunlight.

Case in point: the doorwoman, napping laxly against the loom, godfingers of light stirring through hair, warp, and weft. Quite old now, she felt she was allowed an afternoon nap – she had kept so many bodies, so diligently, so neatly, at such regular intervals. Her honesty was beyond compare.

Section 3. The House Opens. June 2035–July 2036. This section attempts to reconstruct the Opening of the House via my own notes, Savithribaayi's letters and interviews, and news articles.

The rains were heavy and chilling that year (Arhan, 2035) but the doorwoman visited the bodychambers every day. It was too intimate, too dangerous, a denial of her job, entirely wrong. But the doorwoman had killed a rule, and now the bodychambers had been transformed. Her eyes and hands catalogued the bodies and their clothes, eyes especially upon the scarves that hobbled their feet together – threads, weaves, prints, embroidery. The subtle undyed goat hair scarves – originally brown, white, black – were transforming. They had become soft and lush. Flowers rioted across their threads, leaves bloomed like algae after a rain.

The doorwoman had stolen a scarf – previously unthinkable – and now everything felt different.

The doorwoman felt this keenly. In a letter (July 8[tt], 2036) she said to me that of all the humans in the house, only she was attuned to the bodies, to the scars and veins that ran into them. She began to leave the trapdoor open for company.

Her mind was, after all, human.

In an interview after her retirement, the doorwoman described the day she became aware that the House had been filled from the inside. This was the day she threw open the doors:

"I sat at my loom, knee aching. Every time my body faltered, I thought of its body unhalting through the human centuries. I had locked its rollers and treadles in place. Beams and shafts were tied.

"A movement. I saw a glint at the trapdoor.

"Something darted out. A tendril sneaking out and touching the loom. It was crinkled and golden, like a sleeping dragon. It wound around the goat-hair threads strung neatly for the next visitor. More tendrils emerged, as if they were waiting only for the touch of the loom, the warmth of the antechamber."

By noon, the smokepersons would be informed that they were under new management (Arhan) – bodies would no longer be wasted. That was an inefficient practice, now retired. If left unused for more than, say, five years, a body would be repurposed. It was only fair, only a proper use of natural resources.

Many, among them my interviewee 'Abd Al-samad Shirazi, chose to depart by smoke that evening.

Another change: the House of Smoke would be manned by the tall green-and-gold ferns, their plumes nodding on either side of the gate. The retired doorwoman slipped out to the river. A coracle waited for her, bobbing.

Downriver? Upriver? The sky was flat and utterly undomelike. A single dolphin breached the surface and then swam away.

> "I'll return," the doorwoman told the ferns. "In a few years. Tell the loom I want to design my own scarf."
> (Acrostichum, *Yearly Security Report, 2036*, pp. 4)

Conclusions

For humans, the House of Smoke is as it has always been, the perfect holiday, a time away from the slow-grinding wear of the body, from the grim weight of time.

From the botanical view, the House was once seen as empty, sterile. No more. Time, water, sunlight and a million spores have acted upon the House with the surety that characterises the kingdoms plantae and fungi. It is a thing of slow unravelling beauty, a triumph of growth unhindered.

Lastly, this paper offers an observation on the inevitable changes wrought by the scientific method: can you observe a House without sharing yourself with it? I fear that I, Impatiens by name and nature, could not.

Note: All references are embedded in this essay. Pass a tendril over them to read.

The author would like to thank all the guests and the managements, old and new, at the House of Smoke for their contributions, kindness and supportiveness of this project. They would also like to thank the Plant Equality Propagation Foundation for the generous grant that enabled this research.

Tim Jeffreys

The Treachery
of the Heart

Though the house she and Samuel occupied stood on a high crag, isolated and reached only by a narrow road (often blocked by snowfall in wintertime), Maggie sensed that it was a time to be vigilant. Every day, she left the house and walked the same circuit through the hills. Her route looked down, at all points, on the village of Dobcroft, which sat in the basin of the valley. Some days, seeing her donning her coat and pulling on boots, Samuel stared at her like she was mad. 'You're not going out there, are you, dear?' he'd say. 'The rain's coming down at an angle.'

That morning he'd risen before her and gone to his study. As she readied herself to leave the house, she'd called to him, 'I'm going for my walk.' She'd heard the study door open before she reached the front door. He'd come rushing after her with hat, gloves, and scarf, his expression showing only concern. He'd thrust the things at her, saying, 'Here. If you must go wandering about take these. Looks like snow.'

Setting out, she'd thought how it was in his little concerns for her that Samuel showed his love. She thought too that he may have been right; it was cold enough for snow, certainly. The sky had a dark, laden look to it. She wrapped the scarf around the lower half of her face and pulled the hat low on her brow. She wondered if Samuel would decide to take the car down to the village. Probably, he'd want to stock up in case it did snow and the road became impassable. It made her uneasy, thinking he might get stranded, leaving her alone at the house. He went to Dobcroft once or twice a week if the roads were open. She used to go with him, but she hadn't been to the village in weeks. Not since the time they'd gone and found the supermarket closed, police tape cordoning off the pavement outside. Someone had told them it was because there'd been a shooting. Samuel had laughed at this. 'A shooting? Here?' But she'd had an odd feeling, a feeling of being exposed, as if she'd turned around to find someone shining a very bright light into her face. The next time Samuel went to the village, he returned telling her he'd seen police officers going door to door.

'Something's going on down there,' he'd said.

So she walked the same route every day, uncertain of what she was looking for, knowing only that she had to be watchful. If ever she heard the telephone ring, she let Samuel answer it; and at night, before going to bed, she double-checked the locks on the doors and windows. Lying awake, she made little plans in her head of where she'd go, and what she'd take with her if she had to leave the house in a hurry. One time, left alone in the house, she'd gone to the hallway cupboard where Samuel kept the shotgun he used for clay pigeon shooting. There was a box of cartridges on a shelf. She'd held the gun in her hands, examining it until she thought she understood how it worked, then practised loading the cartridges.

During her return home, the sky began to spit snow. Samuel had been right, too, about her needing the hat, gloves, and scarf. She'd underestimated the cold. She pulled up the scarf so that only her eyes were exposed. If Samuel had gone to the village, she hoped he'd got the fire going before he left. She wanted to be in an armchair in front of it already, with a mug of hot tea, watching the snow drift past the window. She started to hurry.

She was within sight of the house when she noticed the young woman – or was it only a girl? – climbing the slope to her right; pale-faced, hugging herself, wearing nothing but a thin dress, her hair flapping like an orange flag. Thinking of Samuel, Maggie ducked down and started to run. But it was too late. The woman had lifted her head and spied her. Maggie straightened up, cursing herself for not bringing the shotgun with her on these walks. But Samuel, of course, wouldn't have allowed that. He'd have wanted to know why. Would've thought her crazier still.

For a few seconds both women froze, facing each other. Maggie, positioned on the crest of the hill, realised she had the advantage. She could run now, before the other woman had time to scramble up the remainder of the slope. She could get inside the house, draw the curtains, and lock all the doors. But she hesitated too long, and the woman moved quick, rapidly closing the gap between them. Maggie's throat tightened. Pretending not to notice that the woman's feet were bare, she nodded and said, 'Uh. Hello.'

The other woman didn't answer. Snowflakes patterned her thick, orange hair. Her cheeks and nose were flushed with cold. Seeing her up close, Maggie thought she'd been right in thinking her only a girl. She was so slim and slight, a slip of nothing really. But there was something calculating in her gaze, something predatory. She walked in a slow circle around Maggie, looking her up and down. Then she halted, blocking the route back to the house, and her eyes narrowed and fixed on Maggie's.

'Cold,' she said, hugging herself tighter and shivering as if to demonstrate. Her teeth chattered.

'Yes it is,' Maggie said, deliberately misunderstanding. 'Haven't you got a coat?'

'No time,' the woman said. 'Had to run.'

Maggie looked towards Dobcroft. *Policemen going door to door,* Samuel had said, the last time he returned from the village. *Christ knows what they're looking for.* She faced the young woman again, careful not to let her gaze stray beyond her to the house.

Stalling for time, she said, 'You'll catch your death out here.'

'That where you live?' the woman said, jerking her head in the direction of the house.

'Yes.' Maggie did her best to keep her voice casual. A snowflake caught on one of her eyelashes, blurring her vision. She blinked it away. 'Me and my husband.'

'Husband?' The woman smirked. Turning, she looked at the house. Following her gaze, Maggie saw smoke pluming from the chimney. So Samuel had lit the fire. But was he still home? Or had he gone to Dobcroft? From where she stood, she couldn't see if the Land Rover was parked on the gravel patch alongside the house.

The woman returned her gaze to Maggie. 'Looks lovely,' she said. 'Nice and cosy. And safe. How long?'

'I'm sorry?'

'How long have you lived there?'

'Since... since I... since we got married.'

The woman's smirk turned into a mocking smile. She leaned forwards. 'And when was that, my love?'

Maggie took a step backwards. 'I don't see that it's any of your...'

The woman startled her by making a quick grab at her scarf, trying to pull it away from her face. Pushing her hands away, Maggie staggered backwards, righting the scarf, ensuring that all but her eyes were covered. The woman lunged at her again, snatching the hat from her head and pulling at the scarf. With a wild cry, Maggie caught hold of the woman's arms. They struggled for a moment. Maggie felt the other's strength pressing against her, the hands clawing at her. The pale, determined face, with blazing eyes and clenched teeth filled her vision. But then she found the strength to spin the woman around and throw her back down the slope. Without pausing, she frantically searched the ground for her hat, at the same time trying to cover her face again with the scarf. But one end had been yanked from inside her coat, and the wind toyed with it. She turned in circles, grasping at the loose end, blinded by the snow which was coming down harder, until she halted, hearing the other woman laughing.

She'd fallen only a short way down the slope before managing to check her tumble. She lay belly down in the grass, her arms crooked at her sides, hands braced against the ground as if at any moment she would spring to her feet. Her head was raised and she glared at Maggie, grinning.

Maggie covered her face with her gloved hands. Too late, though. Too late. She'd been seen. Reeling around in panic, she orientated herself in the direction of the house and started running. A ditch surprised her and she fell. Her chin struck the ground. Her teeth snapped together. Pain. Ice-cold water got inside her boot. Clambering to her feet, dazed, she ran on.

Not until she was metres from the house did she dare look back. She swept her gaze one way, and then the other, searching through the fluttering snow for the woman. Seeing no one, she let out her breath and laughed with relief. But the laughter died in her throat. Someone came over the crest of the low hill ahead of her.

Maggie gasped. 'No.'

Though dressed in the same clothes as the orange-haired woman, the approaching figure was not her. It was an older woman. Dark hair threaded with grey, sagging features. The thin white dress was tight on her, showing the folds of her body.

Dizzied by the pounding of her own heart, Maggie desperately searched her coat pockets for the house keys. Once inside, she closed the door and locked it. She went down the hall as quietly as she could, stopping outside the door to Samuel's study. Putting one ear to the wood, she listened. Her ears were filled with the rushing of her own blood, but she heard nothing else. She would have to knock, or say his name, if she wanted to know for sure if he was inside. But she would not do that. Not yet. She crossed to the hallway cupboard where he kept his shotgun. Taking the gun down, she loaded the cartridges the way she'd practised. Turning back towards the front door, holding the gun in two hands, she heard the sound of a car engine outside.

'No,' she said, shaking her head. 'Samuel.'

She ran to the lounge. The fire blazed in the hearth, and the room was warm. A wing-backed chair and footstool had been arranged close to the fire. Samuel must have moved them there, ready for her return. He really was the sweetest, kindest man she'd ever known. Looking up she saw, in the gilt-framed mirror above the hearth, the same face she'd seen on the figure outside: black hair threaded with grey, sagging features, big frightened eyes. Crossing to the window, she looked out. And gasped. There was Samuel's Land Rover. And there was Samuel, standing beside it with his arm around... with his arm around that other... that...

When the two of them started towards the house, Maggie ducked away from the window. Not knowing what else to do, she rushed up the stairs. She stood on the landing, listening, as they entered the house.

Samuel's voice, incredulous: 'What the hell were you thinking walking around outside dressed like that? Where did you even get that dress? And with nothing on your feet. Maggie... what on Earth?'

Then, a perfect mimicry of her own voice, answering him: 'I'm sorry, darling, I only popped out for a moment. I wanted to see the snow. I don't know what I was thinking.'

Darling? That was a mistake. Maggie never called him 'darling'. Would he notice?

'Come in here,' Samuel said, 'and sit down by the fire.'

Damn it. Maggie clenched one fist, thinking of that other woman sitting in the chair Samuel had set by the fireside. Set by the fireside for *her*. It was supposed to have been for her. She cradled the shotgun in both her hands, wondering what to do. Listening again, she heard Samuel's voice from below.

'I'll make you some tea.'

Footsteps in the hall. When she heard him rattling cups in the kitchen, she crept back down the stairs and into the lounge. The other woman was in the wing-backed chair facing the fire with her bare feet up on the footstool. All Maggie saw was the crown of her head. Raising the shotgun, she crept forwards into the room. She halted when the other woman, without turning around, spoke in a low tone.

'What are you going to do?' A soft chuckle. 'Shoot me?'

Maggie realised she'd forgotten about the mirror above the hearth.

'Get out,' Maggie hissed. 'Get out, or... or I'll blow your head off.'

The woman turned and peered around the chairback. 'And how will you explain that to him?'

'I'll tell him the truth,' Maggie said.

'What?' The woman laughed under her breath again. 'The whole truth?'

'I don't know what you mean.'

The other woman shook her head. 'How long have you been here, living like this? Long enough to forget?'

'Get out. This is *my* home.'

The woman was silent for a few moments. 'Sister,' she said then in a low voice, 'it's him we should get rid of. We can live here together, you and I.'

'I... I'm not your sister.'

'Who are you then? Do you think he knows? Do you think he's known all along?'

Hearing footsteps approaching the room, Maggie crabbed backwards and ducked behind the door. She held her breath, hearing Samuel enter the room.

'Here we are, dear,' Samuel said. 'Nice hot tea. This should do the trick.'

The imposter's voice: 'Thank you, darling. You are kind. Listen, I'm a little peckish now too. You couldn't make me a sandwich, could you? Please. Pretty please.'

'Of course I could. What do you want on it?'

'Oh, anything. Just throw it all on there.'

Wrong. Tuna mayonnaise. Maggie liked tuna mayonnaise.

'I'll see what we have.'

When she heard Samuel retreating down the hall to the kitchen again, Maggie slid out from behind the door. But the other woman must have leapt to her feet the moment Samuel left the room, as she was suddenly there in Maggie's face, grabbing the barrel of the shotgun in two hands, trying to wrench it out of Maggie's hands. In silence, they struggled for possession of the gun.

'Give it to me, sister,' the woman hissed into Maggie's face. 'If you don't want to kill him, I'll do it. We can live here together, you and I. No one has to know. The village isn't safe for our kind anymore. I'll be him, and you keep the woman's face if that's what you want.'

'I don't know what you're talking about,' Maggie hissed back. 'For the last time, I'm not your sister.'

The woman gritted her teeth, pulling at the gun barrel. 'Do you think I can't recognise my own kind? Do you think I can't *smell it*? Do you think I didn't know from the moment I put eyes on you?' Fury darkened the woman's face. She pulled hard on the gun, almost yanking it out of Maggie's hands. 'Give it to me! Do you want to go back to the dark, sister? Huh? Back to the cold? Back to that miserable hole in the ground? Give me the gun. It's him or you. I'm not going back there.'

Without warning, she savagely head-butted Maggie in the face. Pain exploding around her nose, Maggie fell back with a muffled cry. The gun slipped out of her grasp. The other woman had it now. Seeing her swinging around towards the door with a look of triumph on her face, Maggie dived. She and the other woman crashed together to the floor, rolling, struggling, once again fighting for possession of the gun.

Samuel shouted from the kitchen. 'There's some lettuce. Do you want lettuce, dear?'

Maggie and the other woman fell still.

'Yes!' they shouted in unison, before resuming their struggle.

Thinking of the way Samuel cared for her, his tenderness, Maggie found renewed determination, renewed strength. Pushing the other woman down against the floor, she fought to get astride her. Both still had hold of the gun, but Maggie put her weight on top of it, forcing the barrel across the other woman's throat.

'Please...' the woman said. '...sister...'

'I told you,' Maggie said, pressing the shotgun barrel harder into the woman's neck. 'I'm not your bloody sister.'

The other woman's face contorted with a silent scream. Her tongue darted out of her mouth. Her eyes bulged. She made no sound except for a thin rattle. Not until feeling the body beneath her go slack did Maggie stop pressing down. As soon as she did, she clamoured to her feet. Setting the shotgun down behind the door, she returned to the prone woman and, realising there was no time to check for a pulse, she hooked her hands into the woman's armpits and dragged her towards the door. Before leaving the lounge, she leant back and shouted, in as controlled a voice as she could muster, towards the kitchen:

'Toast the bread, will you, dear?'

'What?' Samuel shouted back.

'I said toast the bread for me, please!'

'*Toast* it?' Samuel's incredulous voice came back.

'Yes, I want it toasted.'

'But I've already...'

'What, dear?'

'I've already... never mind. I'll start again.'

Without hesitating, Maggie got her hands back under the woman's armpits and dragged her out of the lounge. The kitchen door was open at the end of the hall. If Samuel should emerge, if he should see her... She pushed the thought from her mind. As silently as she could, she dragged the woman to the front door. Carefully, she drew back the bolts and got the door open. The snow had turned into a blizzard. She could see nothing beyond a few feet in front of her. Dragging the woman out, she dumped her to one side of the door, pleased to think that the snow would quickly cover the body. Dead or alive, it didn't matter. She would deal with it later, perhaps that night when Samuel was asleep. Hurrying back inside, she eased the door shut and rushed to the lounge where she fell down into the wing-backed chair. The heat from the fire felt good. Kicking off her boots, she put her feet up on the footrest just as she heard Samuel's footsteps in the hall.

When he appeared with the sandwich, he stood over her with a bewildered look.

'My god, Maggie,' he said. 'Your nose is bleeding.'

'Is it?' She touched a finger to her lip, saw blood on it. 'So it is.'

'Here,' Samuel said, taking a handkerchief from his pocket and handing it to her. 'Whatever happened?'

'Nothing.' She dabbed at her nose with the handkerchief. 'It's just one of those things.'

He looked along her body. 'And you got changed?'

'Of course!' Realising she sounded half-crazed, she took a deep breath to calm herself. 'You didn't think I was going to sit around in a thin little dress all day, did you? On a day like this?'

'What I don't understand,' Samuel said, in a reprimanding tone, 'is why you were wearing that thin little dress in the first place.'

'I found it in the back of my wardrobe, that's all, and I was trying it on when I saw the snow coming down and I rushed outside to see it. I do love the snow. Don't look so bewildered, dear. I wasn't thinking. That's all.'

It was a poor explanation, at which Samuel narrowed his eyes, but he didn't question her further. She often wondered if he knew the truth. She'd been careful, and had spent some time watching his wife, the real Maggie Harris, studying her mannerisms and modes of speech before that day when she'd seen Samuel climb into his Land Rover and drive away, and she'd finally approached the house. She remembered how Maggie Harris' face had looked when she answered the door. Surprised, but amiable.

Can I help you?

She'd buried the body in a shallow grave far out on the moor, in a spot even she couldn't have found again, and had installed herself at the house before Samuel returned. She would do the same thing with the body outside if it was still there by nightfall. *Back to the dark, sister. Back to the cold.* She had a good thing here. It was cosy and safe, just like the woman had said when they faced each other out on the hillside. And she had a man who loved her. She wasn't going to make any foolish missteps like calling him "darling". Things that would make him suspicious. And if a knock should come on the front door, she would escape out the back. Who knows where she would go then, what face she would choose. She would be sad to leave Samuel, true. A man so doting was not easy to find.

Maggie watched the thick snowflakes cascading past the window. Judging by the way it was coming down out there, there'd be no knock on the door for a few weeks at least. Plenty of time to think. Plenty of time to make a plan.

He remained standing, looking quizzically at her. 'Are you sure you're alright, dear?'

She looked at him, standing so tall over her. He remained a handsome man, despite his age, with a full head of hair, perfectly white. He was in his seventies now and so, she remembered, was she. Never once had he asked her why she didn't look a day over fifty-five.

And as for that miserable hole in the ground. Ha! That miserable hole in the ground was a long time ago. She'd lived here long enough to forget, yes, and indeed she almost had. She hardly thought about her beginnings anymore, or wondered where they were, the others. It was another life. But if ever there was a time to remember it was a time like this, when she sat in front of the blazing fire, with her feet up on the stool and a mug of hot tea in her hand, watching snow fall past the window.

Turning to Samuel, she showed him a smile. The way he looked at her now, head cocked, brow knit, made her wonder if he did know; if he had known all along. Perhaps he preferred things this way. After all, she was nothing if not malleable. Unlike the real Maggie Harris, she could mould herself to suit his needs.

'Darling,' she said, testing him, watching his face. She saw not a flicker. 'Don't fret. I'm perfectly fine.'

Claire Watson

We Came Travelling

'Something is bound to happen,' Jones says, taking a prophetic drag from his cigarette. He exhales, sending wayward clouds of smoke towards the heavens. Up, to where the sky is turning peach, and the stars are poking through what little blue remains. Leaning in the stone doorway, he hides from the setting sun.

'Something, somewhere, sometime...' he goes on, scuffing his shoes against the wall and its peeling paint.

You crouch in the heart of the patio. It catches the sunlight, so that every stone is a sheet of gold. The light is soft on your skin, blurs your edges. Cigarettes and joints trail along the flagstone. Out from a gap, a dandelion rears its head. You cup it between your palms. Inside, a party has just begun. Out here, there is life, as there always has been.

'Something is always happening,' you say, stroking the dandelion. Pollen spills into the hatch marks of your skin.

You stand to meet his gaze. 'But you're speaking cosmically.'

In the same moment that Jones shakes his head at you, laughter erupts from the kitchen window.

'If you mean the aliens, then yeah, I'm speaking cosmically.'

'But I agree with you. Something is bound to happen.' You look out, down the hill to where your university lies. 'I think it's already started.'

From here, you can see the ring burned across the stone campus. They found you in the middle of it, after the black-out. Since, you've had no peace from the wannabe journal-ists shoving phones in your face. You tell them all the same thing: you passed out.

One moment you were walking home from the library and the next you were lying face down on the cold earth. It was nothing strange, only an accident.

'Think you'll get abducted?' Jones asks and sticks his hands in his pockets. 'Abductions happen all the time. You should watch the news.'

'Won't be so coy when they start probing you.'

'Quite like a bit of probing, actually.'

You remember how the darkness held you. It wasn't a blackout. You'd stepped beyond the threshold and the world closed in on you. It gripped you in a pulsating claw. Pure energy writhed down your spine.

Look up, it asked. *See the stars.*

In the darkness, you forgot where your body ended and the world began. Putting your hands forward, you stum-bled towards something tangible, something earthly. When you fell you couldn't feel the difference between the stone beneath you, and the skin around you. Electricity swirled from your temporal lobe and down to your toenails. A voice screamed inside your hippocampus, begging you to look up.

There is no ground. There is no Earth. There is only this.

When you looked up, you saw holes pricked in the dark expanse. Where there were once stars, there were only slits refusing light. The darkness said, *look here, at the singularities. These are lives. These are empty. These are alive.*

You were weightless in the dark.

There is so much fear inside you, little one. Be not afraid. We come in peace. A seam in reality tore open, and in flooded the world with its strange people staring down at you.

You reach past Jones to tear paint from the wall. He watches as it digs into the flesh beneath your nails. There's that sound again: laughter from the kitchen. You follow it to find strangers draped over white countertops, their glasses shining in the fluorescence.

'We humans have been sitting pretty for far too long, thinking we're the only ones out here.'

You don't look at Jones as you speak. Instead, you watch the group. A woman pulls open the fridge, to hide her face as her smile crumbles. She stands in a mandorla of cartons, bottles and jars rattling in the fridge door. A tear slips down her foundation-slick skin.

You drop the shard of paint and see the lacework of grime coating its underside. The woman pulls back her smile and rejoins the group.

'We should head in,' you say, turning back to Jones. 'People might think we got abducted.'

A harsh wind skids against your cheeks, pulling you to turn around. *Before you go*, it says. *Look down, down into the creasing valleys.*

You obey, to find the golden-lit buildings imbued with living. *Look past the river as it slips through the city, past the university and its extraterrestrial bruise. Hear how the river gushes over rocks and squeezes between grassy banks.*

Look, the darkness says. *Look across the valley.*

You see the abandoned asylum watching over the town, its face as red as Jones'. *Do you see the houses with their streetlights?*

Cars climb up the hill to drive out of view. All those little lights. At night, the world becomes a mirror of the stars. All those little lights shine in the indigo sky, each one implying a different kind of life. All those little lights, near and far. The wind howls as it swoops down the hill and across the river, up to where it meets your face. It pulls your hair across your eyes.

'Wait,' you call out. Jones rests his hand on the door. You try to pull your hair back into place. 'Do I look alright?'

He steps down. His toes kick against yours. He toys with your fringe, your eyes level with his mouth.

'You look perfect.'

He guides you back inside, hand splayed against your shoulder. Over the threshold, and into the party. You let him steer you through the darkness, past the unfamiliar faces and their unfamiliar laughs.

Something is bound to happen, and yet nothing does.

Not while you sit on the couch with a glass of wine warming between your thighs. Your knee brushes against a man's ripped skinny jeans. Nothing happens while his leg hair pokes through the fronds of fraying thread as he spreads his legs wide, forcing you to fold into yourself. Not while your elbows are crashing into your rib cage, your lungs swelling as you force out fake laugh after fake laugh.

There are black spots in the universe, beyond the maws of black holes, where stars cannot swim. Voids of nothingness, floating through space. Darker than the end. Darker than the moment your eyes stop recording, your lips stop tasting, and your fingers stop feeling. When your brain pauses, never to process again.

And there is a black spot, here in this living room. Where there is a man with orange and rum staining his breath. The droplets like beads threaded through his attempt at a beard. He yawns in your face and asks you about the world and the aliens from above. You shrug and answer that there is nothing out there. Nothing tangible. Nothing that your human minds could possibly grasp.

He looks at you, as though your skin is green and your eyes are stretching up your forehead.

You shake your head and give a smile, 'Nothing. I passed out. I saw nothing.' He stands. Mutters something about refilling his drink but goes out onto the patio, where he starts stealing cigarettes.

It's too bright inside to watch him stumble through the dark. All you can see in the window are the flashing fairy lights buzzing around the living room. They flicker along the rainbow, each bulb confiscating the view of night. You twist and cup your hands around your eyes to stare up at the sky and for a second your body is somewhere else, floating high into the stratosphere. You hear someone laugh, hear the couch squeak under your knees, and you're brought back down.

Instead, you watch the party in reflection. There's a blur of people sitting on the couches, clutching their drinks as they shout over the music. Each person, each beautiful stranger, contains a marvel of life that you can barely comprehend. Each laugh has been moulded by at least two decades of life – lives that have been running alongside yours yet never, until this moment, touching.

You find Jones' face, his lips rippling around a laugh. He clutches the leather sofa like it's the only thing stopping him from floating up into the stars. Beside him sits the girl from the fridge. She doesn't speak, only nods along to whatever it is that Jones says.

In his reflection, the words come out backwards.

Beside her is another man, who Jones is really speaking to. His laugh is a hiccup, like a gravitational wave blipping through the unknown. Jones introduced you once, but you've since lost his name.

Behind them both is a large patch of black mould. You imagine walking towards it, climbing over Jones and the girl from the fridge and the man whose name you can never remember, and peeling back the stained paint. Behind it would be another world, made of that warm darkness that held you once before.

Inside it, voices whisper, and their whispers are worth listening to.

Instead, you stand and move into the kitchen. Though your glass is full, you open the fridge and grab another drink. You let yourself cry a single tear, and then you smile and stand in the centre of the empty room. The light is off. The glow of the moon trickles through the glass. The countertop glitters beneath a sea of squashed aluminium. Like anorthosite. Like space rock.

Something, somewhere, sometime. You hold out your arms and wait for something to happen. When it doesn't, you down your drink and try once more.

Something will, something whispers.

The floorboards of the hallway creak under the heavy saunter of Jones and his leather boots that you've only seen him take off once. You watch him through the crack of the doorway, as he staggers into the hall. His hand rests on the girl from the fridge's back. She shakes and falls against his chest.

As he leads her upstairs, Jones whispers, 'It'll be alright. You're okay. We'll get you some space.'

The man whose name you can't remember bursts into the kitchen, flicks on the light. He jumps when you say, 'Hey.'

He brushes past you, clunking against the kitchen tiles as he rushes for the sink. He wears boots like Jones'.

He turns the tap onto full pressure, and it screams against the basin. You watch how his hands shake, as water sprays across his knuckles.

He flicks off the light and leaves.

You sip your wine. Feel its purple touch mingling with your red lips. The stairs creak. Jones' leather boots march over your head.

He took them off after he held you, after he pushed you down and climbed into bed. Beneath the covers. Your flesh cold against his, a fever broiling inside his skin. He was barefoot when you trembled beside him. He thanked you. Outside the moon was reclining in its crescent, and you were only thankful that he hadn't drawn the curtains.

You told everyone you were walking back from the library. What else could you have said?

Look up, asks the darkness. *Towards the stippled ceiling.*

'Is it happening now?' you ask, your voice a crumb caught in the back of your throat. *Yes.*

'Is it happening again?'

Yes, but we will keep you safe.

The footsteps grow lighter, grow in numbers, grow in energy. Stuttering back and forth. A glass clinks. There is a bang, muffled by a thin layer of carpet. How did you get wine on your blouse? Look at the fuchsia feathering out from your breast. Press your hand against it, as though to stop the bleeding. Watch your fingertips change colour. There is a puddle of wine growing on the kitchen tiles – how did it get there? You are alone.

Plunge your finger between your lips. Suck on the bitter taste. Envision the wine staining your throat, and briefly, envision your insides being filled by a deep, violet ooze. Take another mouthful, take it.

'Make it stop, please,' you sputter through tears. They slip between your lips, and taste dissolves into the background. It becomes the static playing behind your ears. There is only this.

We cannot intervene. We are so very sorry.

The lights, the oven, the microwave – everything – flashes to life. The world is noisy and bright. Everything is shaking, buzzing, and everyone inside the house is screaming, laughing.

'Is there something out there?' You collapse to your knees, your thighs soaking up the spilt wine.

Yes, yes, yes. We are here. We will protect you.

Everything short-circuits. The world plunges into darkness. It wraps around you like an old blanket. It takes you into its arms and strokes your hair. It smells of your mother's skin and freshly spilt blood, trickling from your knee. You crumble against the tiles, into her embrace. You hold the empty wine glass against your heart, as we hold you against ours.

It'll be alright. You're okay. We'll get you some space.

You fall into the stars, sobbing.

Forget the cold ground against your skin. The sobs from upstairs. His rough hands. And forget the frailty of your bones. How you cried as he clenched your skin. Forget the shortness of your breath. The sweat in your hair. Be not afraid, we say. Be not afraid, we've got you.

You will cry and you will dry your eyes. You will remember how to be in this body, and you will remember how to be in this world. That these stars, that these stories, that these lives, are all yours. We are sorry we could not keep you safe. You are sorry you could not keep her safe. There is as much guilt as there is fear in this vast world.

Feel our hands comb through your hair. We will undo these knotted strands. We cannot undo the past. There, there, little one.

When the lights come back, you stay in darkness. You rise to your feet and move towards the doorway. There waits the girl from the fridge.

She stands like a gilded spaceman, gaping at the world she thought she knew. She steps down from the spacecraft, from the stairs. Onto the dusty moon, and into the narrow hall. Light swells against the front door's frosted glass, forming a halo behind her skull. Her shadow weaves down the hall, to fall against your face. There, in the light, you see patches of her skin steadily growing violet. Yes, something has happened. You take one small step towards her, and then another.

Phil Cummins

The Molecular Theory of Horses

Sipping his stout, the proprietor of Brasil's Family Butchers contemplated the sad decline of Tully's Pub. A proper old-fashioned boozer at one time, doling out pints of porter to hard-working tradesmen and farmers happily absorbed in daily banter, some eejit had decided a pool table and pop music were essential to its evolution. The next thing you knew the place was a magnet for pimply young bucks squaring up to one another with vigorously chalked pool cues and skimpily clad young ones trying to catch their eye as they hoovered vapes and thumbed texts into mobiles, either sex ensuring a steady flow of coins into the jukebox. Maurice Brasil sighed and shook his big corpulent head disapprovingly. He didn't really mind the sight of the girleens for in truth he was a bit of a lech, but the lively exuberance of youth irritated him, and the din spewing out of the juke – some whiny-voiced creature pleading with the world to go easy on her – was nothing less than an aural torment to him.

Brasil sat scowling at the end of the bar, a portly man the wrong side of 50, all rubbery lips and jowls, with drooping eyes of the heavy-lidded sort set beneath a broad sweaty forehead. A threadbare combover was scraped over his florid scalp and the smells of his trade, of sour sawdust and greasy tripes, rolled off him like an organic fog, though he'd long since ceased to notice such things. He'd inherited the butcher shop from his late father, also christened Maurice but known to all and sundry as Mossy. A Tully's regular back in the day with a reputation for meanness, Mossy's reputed ability to peel a grape in his pocket was the stuff of legend. And just like his father, it could be said that Brasil himself was rarely in too much of a hurry to pay for his round, whilst no one in living memory had ever witnessed the collection basket gain weight in his vicinity during mass of a Sunday. Combining these unsavoury character traits with a clatter of financial woes and the fact that his wife, a Northern woman of fiery disposition, had fecked off two years previous with their twins, Paudie and Ailbhe, rightly led one to conclude that the poor man had fuck all going for him. When asked, Brasil would routinely claim that Brigid had simply returned to care for her elderly mother above in Dungannon, although local gossip had it she'd dusted off her maiden name and taken up with a hotelier from Bundoran. On the plus side, their eldest lad, Emmett, had remained living with him to help run the shop, although in Brasil's view his son exhibited no great interest in the trade and couldn't tell a pork chop from a streaky rasher. Emmett, he sometimes felt, would've been more useful clacking balls with the brainless yokes strutting their stuff around the nearby pool table.

In the space of twenty minutes, the barman had twice engaged Brasil to enquire smilingly if he was ready for a fresh pint, attempting on both occasions to strike up conversation on matters of vital importance to the latest Premier League fixtures. Brasil refused the former and expressed complete indifference to the latter, prompting the barman to redirect his attention to the careful slicing of lemons at the other end of the bar. It was only when Brasil spotted the barman striding purposefully towards him a third time with a face on him like a jug of sour piss that he knew it was time to drink up.

'That cunt, Ward, is after rocking up out the back,' snapped the barman, his mouth a tight pucker of revulsion. 'He says *you* arranged to meet him here, Maurice. Him and his brothers have been barred out of here for life, as well you know. Caused us no end of fucking grief, that shower. You may go outside to jaw with him, but don't linger.'

Nodding resignedly, Brasil downed the dregs of his pint before trudging out back to see a man about a horse.

Ward was a befreckled, carrot-headed slab of a man, lumpishly assembled and with thick-set arms ending in mitts the size of ham hocks. A man well used to being eyeballed suspiciously, a wild pugnacious aura seemed to peel off him. He and Brasil negotiated over the price of the horse, its owner wanting rid of it pronto, having recently acquired a younger model. Spit-soaked palms were finally pressed and the animal delivered in the nocturnal hours to the back of Brasil's shop. Hard-ridden and banjaxed, purchased for a song, Brasil personally dispatched the poor nag to the hereafter, allowing its butchered carcass to hang for a spell and tenderise before carving and mincing it up to supplement his regular range of meats. He'd decided Emmett, with a gob on him like the Mersey Tunnel, was best kept in the dark about such clandestine arrangements.

As the days unfolded into weeks, Brasil noticed a curiously pleasant uptick in his trade. His meat pies and lasagnas, rustled up daily by Anastasia, a temperamental Moldovan woman who seemed to know her way around a double-oven Aga, were flying off the shelves. His marinated meatballs rolled out the door as quick as you like and his burger trays were bare by lunchtime. Nobody seemed any the wiser to the fact that if his mince could talk it would moo and whinny at the same time, the arrangement with Ward having led to further covert transactions which included another two elderly trotting horses, a 14-hand cob, and three donkeys. He'd had no choice, he told himself. Money was tight. Economies had to be made if the shop was to remain a going concern, health and safety be damned. Discount German supermarkets with their tacky centre aisle get-ups and loss leaders were sprouting up like weeds all over the Midlands, drawing customers like flies to shite, leaving small town merchants like himself scrambling for crumbs. And soaring beef costs saw Hackett's Abattoir out beyond Tullamore riding him from every angle on price, forcing him to source cheaper alternatives. (The fact that the barman in Tully's was brother-in-law to the abattoir's owner, Donie Hackett, a psychologically unstable crook of the highest order with whom Brasil was unfortunately required to do business, constituted another factor in Tully's sad decline, he reasoned.)

It was a lively conversation some days later between two customers, Lar Carey and Gertie Loughran, concerning the unusual misfortune that had befallen Tadgh Tyrell and his wife, that hinted some strangeness was afoot. The mere mention of Josie Tyrell had caused Brasil's ears to prick up and his blood to quicken. Beef to the heel, Josie's magnificent haunches had long been admired by him whenever she stopped into the shop to procure some stewing mince and the makings of a fry, her voluptuous contours regularly fueling his fevered imagination during many a solitary late night hand shandy.

'Poor Josie,' lamented Gertie. 'Her nerves must be shattered.'

Carey nodded his agreement. 'In pure shock the woman is, with himself knocked senseless above in Naas Hospital in a coma.'

When Brasil enquired as to Tadgh's circumstances, Carey explained that, during an outing to Punchestown Racecourse the day before, Tyrell and the wife were watching the mounts parading by towards the starting gate when he took a sudden notion to dip without warning beneath the safety barrier. As if drawn by some uncanny animal magnetism, he then ran up to a passing mare, reefed up its tail and commenced sniffing at its muscular hindquarters with unseemly enthusiasm.

'G'way to fuck!' spluttered Brasil, all thoughts of Josie Tyrell's arse temporarily in abeyance.

'Gospel,' said Carey. 'Of course, the horse wasn't having any of it. The poor thing bucked and drop-kicked Tyrell an unmerciful fucken smack in the head. Knocked the stupid gobshite into next week.'

'Mrs Tyrell must have gotten a woeful shock,' said Brasil.

'Oh, a right scare and no mistake. But sure that wasn't the worst of it,' said Carey, winking. 'I have it on good author-ity he'd a boner on him a mile long when he landed.'

'Oh, poor Josie,' repeated a now red-faced Gertie in the process of blessing herself. 'She must've been mortified.'

Quite so, they all agreed. Mortified.

An uneasy chill ran through Brasil then. *Surely not*, he thought, guiltily. *It couldn't be due to that. Could it?*

The following day saw Anastasia arrive into work in a per-ceptibly filthier mood than normal as she donned her apron. An energetic woman of fetchingly robust proportions, Brasil had learned early on to keep his distance after she'd threat-ened to take his eye out with a paring knife in response to his dropping the hand on her during her first week in the job. Thereafter, theirs became a working relationship strict-ly underpinned by social distancing as the kitchen exten-sion to the rear of the house became her exclusive domain during the daylight hours; Brasil gave her a wide berth and his customers expressed contentment with the quality of her cuisine. Dropping the day's supplies out to the kitchen, he quickly deduced that the woman was clearly in no mood to be fucked around with as she viciously pummeled a large potful of boiled spuds with the masher in preparation for a batch of Shepherd's pies. The normally brisk domesticity of the kitchen was dialled up to near industrial levels of tension. Dishes clattered and oven doors slammed as Anastasia thundered about the space, muttering what Brasil could only assume were Moldovan swear words of the most vulgar sort. He genuinely feared the Aga doors wouldn't survive the punishment.

'Everything alright, Stasie?' Brasil meekly enquired, keeping near to the kitchen door.

'NO! Everything *NOT* alright!'

'What's after happening? Something up with Oleg?'

'Do not mention that *useless* husband!' With a well-known affinity for the grog, Oleg was often to be spotted half-cut on payday, staggering the well-worn path between boozer and bookies. Anastasia continued to vent. 'Drinking. And puking into toilet. All night!'

'I gather he was out on the lash then?' said Brasil.

'Not pints! I find him leaning over with head dipped down into old stone horse trough outside our cottage drinking the rainwater.' Brasil winced at the mention of this, having personally watered that very trough no small number of times himself whilst staggering home after a skinful. Anastasia went on to complain that her husband had taken to vaulting over the gate of a nearby stud farm in the mornings to go chasing around the paddock after the yearlings, pausing occasionally to pull up a few blades of grass to nibble on.

Brasil suddenly felt like a small, trapped animal and his breath caught and his bowels tightened as a dizzying rush of adrenaline suddenly charged through him, and his mind performed vigorous computations as it strained to make sense of these bizarre revelations of horse-like behaviour. He didn't believe in coincidences and slept poorly that night as worms of suspicion began to wriggle and writhe in the deepest parts of his brain.

Brasil's shop wouldn't have been what you'd call fancy, but it was *his* personal place of business, a daily court of operations where he busied himself trading in the flesh of domesticated animals. His little kingdom. The following morning, however, he wore his crown heavily for his night's sleep had been plagued by bad dreams and wild visions, visions of thundering hooves and snorting nostrils and billowing manes, and of a corruption of natural laws that saw his dream horses spontaneously erupt into unbounded atoms and molecules now free to seek new embodiments whilst still imbued with a remembrance of their previous equine manifestation. He faced into his day's work feeling jaded and jittery, unable to shake the feeling that something of his recent actions had somehow seeped like damp into the townsfolk, warping their very natures. Mentally deciding then and there to end his arrangement with Ward, he found himself cheering up to no end and better able to devote himself to the obsequious bonhomie he pedalled daily with his patrons. But as the day wore on, strands of conversation would occasionally spin out from the unguarded chit-chat that weaved between his customers and needle him, constantly reminding him of his dilemma.

'...chomped his way through a full box of Granny Smiths when I had me back turned, so he did. And he wouldn't have thanked you for an apple before today. Poor gobshite is buckled with the wind now and has the whole shagging house stank out of it. He's like the 18 fucken 12 overture.'

'...thin as a rail, that fella. Sure he couldn't be anything but a jockey. Attracta says he's hung like a stallion but that now he's after taking up with some slapper from Ballyvaughan. She gives it a month before he comes crawling back to her.'

'...oh, a right pair on her and no mistake. She wouldn't fall flat on her face, I'll tell ye. As big as her mammy's. The absolute cut of her. It's true what they say: trot filly, trot foal.'

'...came in at 7 to 2 in Leopardstown yesterday. One of Gordon Elliott's. Sure he's going around like a dog with two dicks. Tells me he only had a hundred on it. And d'ye think I'll see a penny of it? Fat chance.'

'...Rubber Bandits how are ye! Fuck your Honda Civic, I've a horse outside, fuck your Subaru...'

Brasil's brain hummed like a well-poked wasp's nest. All this horsey talk was surely some cruel form of chastisement being doled out by the universe, a celestial scratched record designed to drive him demented.

'...built like a Clydesdale, that lad. The guts of a hundred kilos and more. Prop-forward for Belvedere at the minute.

An absolute bruiser, but he still has a good gallop on him when he has space to move. Sure he'll play for Leinster someday. Nothin' surer.'

'...back in the saddle again. I'll tell you what, but that over-the-counter Viagra stuff is the absolute biz. Gives you a right horn. Have you given it a go yourself?'

'...horsey, horsey, don't you stop, just let your feet go clippity clop, the tail goes swish and the wheels go round, here we go we're homeward bound,' Emmett was singing cheerily over the counter to one of the Banthorpe-Kennedy twins wriggling in its mother's arms as he bagged her up several generous fistfuls of cocktail sausages destined for consumption at the Lions Club whist drive later that evening.

This was all getting a bit too much for Brasil.

'This isn't Top of the feckin' Pops, lad!' Brasil barked, roughly shouldering Emmett aside. 'Get out back to the cold room and top us up for more cocktail sausages. We're running low on chicken wings and fillets as well. D'ye think you can bloody well manage that?'

From behind his father's back, Emmett shot Georgina Banthorpe-Kennedy one of his by now well-practised "apologies-for-the-aulfella-but-he-woke-up-this-morning-with-a-bramble stuck-up-his-hole" looks before waggling his fingers at the goo-eyed child and retreating.

'Sure he's grand, Mr Brasil,' said Georgina. 'Wasn't he entertaining Nathan here for me.' Still grumbling as Georgina departed, Brasil came face to face with Muriel Cantwell. A retired local school principal known for her harsh deployment of the righteous tongue-lashing towards pupils and parents alike, Muriel possessed a gimlet stare on her that could loosen the guts of a mass murderer. 'You might go a bit handier with that lad now, Maurice,' said Muriel, her eyes narrowed to reproachful slits. 'There's wasters the same age as your Emmett swaggering about this town waiting for dole day and I wouldn't give you tuppence for them. He's a grand lad, head and shoulders above most of them, and much smarter than you think. You might give him some credit.'

'Now, Ms Cantwell,' snapped Brasil, 'I'd ask that you stick that nosey feckin' beak of yours into somebody else's business and kindly keep it out of mine. I think I know my own son a bit better than you and a foot in the arse is exactly what he needs from time to time to keep his mind on the job.'

Muriel shot him a look then, one normally reserved for the sudden unwelcome detection of a nearby fart during mass. 'Well now, haven't you turned into the right grubby little tyrant, Maurice Brasil,' she hissed, her tone scorching the very air between them. 'Mossy'd be dead proud of the job he did on you. I only hope to God you haven't managed to rub off too much on poor Emmett. It'd be the ruination of him to take after you. He'd have been far better off getting well away from here with Brigid when she finally took her leave of you.'

Cut to the quick, mortification rinsed Brasil's cheeks as the door swung to a close behind Muriel. Knuckles bunched white against the cold stainless of the countertop to steady himself, he exhaled a dismal groan into the now empty shop. 'Well that's me well feckin' told, isn't it?' he sighed.

Dark shadows clustered like treacherous crows in the laneway to the rear of Brasil's shop, the night's normal shush marred by the sound of angry voices. Ward's displeasure at the unilateral cessation of their business arrangement was palpable, his eyes shimmering menacingly as he clenched and unclenched his brawny fists. Violence was a distinct possibility. 'You haven't heard the last of this,' he snarled. Swallowing noisily, Brasil managed to hold his ground as Ward lumbered off into the darkness, fiercely relieved to see the back of him.

Trouble of a different sort, however, would shortly darken his door, for it was two days later when Emmett fetched up black and blue in Midland Regional with a fractured pelvis, four cracked ribs and a broken collar bone. Dispatched on foot that morning to deliver the weekly victuals up to the parochial house, witnesses claimed the lad had inexplicably paused next to a parked Land Rover and, setting down his goods, proceeded to unhitch its trailer from the back. According to local pensioner, Art Hickey: 'The next thing you know, he's tearing off down the hill of Main Street hauling the bloody trailer after him like a sort of carriage and roaring GIDDY UP T'FUCK! It was like he was possessed. The poor lad was fairly travelling when his foot caught by accident in a pothole and he went sprawling arse over tit, the trailer rolling on over him like he was a bag of sticks.'

The too-warm air of the hospital hung heavy with the bitter smells of carbolic and suffering. Brasil clasped his son's bandaged hand as Emmett lay cloaked in a fog of analgesia amidst a confusion of tubes and drips and plaster casts and blinking LEDs. Reduced now to a blubbering heap, Muriel Cantwell's shaming words still raw, Brasil wallowed in self-loathing.

This was all his fault, he told himself, all down to his own arrogant crookery. He couldn't even blame Ward for this. He needed to make things right. And so, the following morning found him sitting in the drab, fluorescent lit interview room of the local cop shop staring at walls the colour and texture of Ready Brek and wishing desperately for something stronger to stiffen the tea in his mug and help loosen his tongue.

'Take your time now, Mr Brasil,' said Sergeant Bermingham. 'Sure, there's no big rush. It's clear to me that you've something weighing heavily on your mind, perhaps something relating to your son's unfortunate accident yesterday.' Bermingham oozed empathy, the biro patiently hovering in readiness above the notebook waiting to record Brasil's narrative. Pulling in a deep breath then, he ploughed ahead with his story and inside of five minutes all traces of the guard's compassionate façade had disintegrated.

'HORSES! Are you fucken telling me you've been butchering HORSES and turning them into mince and whatnot to sell to the townsfolk? All to save a few bob? What sort of a thundering fucken eejit are ye?'

'And the occasional donkey,' added Brasil, meekly. Full disclosure, he felt, was the best policy at this point.

Bermingham's face burned beet red as spittle flew madly from his lips, the biro now clasped in the manner of a stabbing implement. 'Are you even remotely aware of the aggro this nonsense caused the ministers above in Leinster House a few years back? Driven into a frenzy with this shite, so they were. A dirty little crook is all you are, mister. A fucken disgrace. And we a horse nation! I'm going to see you get hung, drawn and quartered for this. You're finished.' Bermingham looked poised to lunge across the table and throttle him, but somehow managed to control himself. Rising abruptly instead, he hopped the biro off the table with considerable ferocity before storming from the interview room.

Brasil sat listening to the slamming of doors and the muffled howls of disgust beyond the interview room, for how long he couldn't be sure. The normal flow of time seemed to have thickened to treacle as he stared into the brackish depths of his mug. An unfamiliar stream of calmness now washed through him and he felt strangely untethered. It was only a matter of time, he reckoned, before the health and safety boyos would swoop in with their CSI swabs and their sample bags and their fancy gene machines. For his son's sake, Brasil would cooperate and take full blame. His estranged wife was almost certainly en route down from Bundoran and gearing up to ate him without salt for making a complete cack of everything. And no doubt the good sergeant would return before too long to read him his rights.

Such is the rich tapestry of small town life. Folks continued to talk about these bizarre events long after the closure of Brasil's Family Butchers and the incarceration of its owner for a spell. Perhaps it was a gust of wind from far off Zanzibar, some mused, or perchance the orbit of Venus had carried it into the shadow of Jupiter. A quare ripple effect of climate change was also offered up as a possibility, one that gave birth to a noxious germ of some description that hitched a ride on the back of a migrating swallow and which was capable of mutating human behaviour. The engagement of foreign agencies and bad actors in chemical warfare through the local water supply was also widely advocated among the older patrons at Tully's. Regardless of the cause, the ministers above in Leinster House were said to be taking the matter very seriously.

Corinne Engber

Satellite Office

It starts, like everything, in February. The day of the kickoff
– February 6th, circled in red on her desk calendar. A measly
week before Valentine's Day, and she is doodling little hearts
in the margins of her legal pad instead of listening. Outside
her office's bay window, the day is grimy and dreary, awful
enough that her wife set up the SunSet™ Vitamin D lamp on
her desk before leaving for work.

'Drink lots of water, and don't forget to stretch,' Viv said,
and then, redundantly, 'I love you.'

On one monitor, her supervisor is speaking: thanking the
assemblage for their presence and punctuality, pulling up
the presentation's first slide, but Viv is what she's thinking
of. Viv on the sectional, Viv in the shower, Viv at the kitchen
island eating grapefruit. Patient Viv, who never gets angry
when she can't get out of bed, who, when the anxiety makes
her vomit, sits on the bathroom floor beside her with cold

towels and ginger chews. To be loved by such a woman and not to think of her! She can't bear to conjure it.

On the other monitor, a folder of last year's schematics in white and blue, familiar as the veins beneath each wrist. That project had been far from her first, but easily her finest: the stunning product of countless sleepless nights and terrifying bouts of imposter syndrome. Who was she, she'd sobbed into Viv's arms, to spearhead the design of such an exquisite piece of tech? Who was she to be taken seriously, to speak at length about the project to such *important* people?

'You're my brilliant wife,' Viv said. 'If they won't take you seriously, *make them.*'

And she had, in the end. The project launched on time and with it, a landmark fiscal year with dividends and demand far exceeding even her supervisor's expectations. The success earned her a hefty raise and a permanent spot at the table, which she had retained even after the later setbacks. The night after the launch, Viv took her out for tapas. 'See?' she said through a mouthful of mushrooms and chive-speckled goat cheese. 'Absolutely nothing to worry about.'

There had been, of course, but there was no way Viv could have known that. She was sweet, savvy but ultimately too generous in her expectations of others. Who could begrudge her the impulses of a kind heart?

This is what she's thinking about when it starts. So small at first, compared to what it becomes. She doesn't even notice it, really, and neither do the twelve tiled faces peering through their little screens. At least, not until she clicks the spacebar and her fingertip comes away sticky.

A hangnail, most likely. A piece of dead skin torn from her cuticle by the fibers of her chunky sweater. It barely registers as an injury – more an inconvenience than anything else. Without shifting her gaze from the screen, she takes a tissue from the box beside her monitor and presses it to her thumbnail. Everything proceeds as normal.

She waits until the meeting goes dark to peel back the tissue. A stamp of blood is baked into the ridged nail, already dried brown. Had she been picking again? Beneath the smear, the skin around her nail bed is healthy and unbroken. The same is true for all the others. To keep herself from ruminating, she wraps the offending finger in a bandage, but by the time Viv returns from her rented remote workstation, the edge is already coming up.

Viv doesn't need to work, not really, but she does anyway. She says she gets bored otherwise, that wandering through the house all day – even a house like this one – makes her feel claustrophobic. 'Absence makes the heart grow fonder,' she says lightly, almost joking. 'Besides, I want to contribute, and being gone means I can enjoy you that much more when I'm here.'

And they do enjoy each other, when the mood strikes. Best to take advantage before the project's true beginning, before she's stretched so thin she can't breathe. They fall, gasping like teenagers, onto fresh sheets, pillows carefully plumped by people they both backpedal from doorways to avoid. Viv's face awash in sunset, pink and periwinkle, her hair a rich halo. Red lipstick smudges at the corners of her mouth. Behind her back, the damp, fraying bandage scrapes her shoulder blade.

Afterwards, dappled in the dark, Viv draws the wounded hand to her lips. 'Did you cut yourself?' she asks innocently.

'Nope. Just a hangnail, I think.'

'Hm.' She laces the fingers in hers to inspect them, turning them this way and that to catch the meager light. 'Seems like a lot of blood.'

It is. In the bathroom, the bandage comes off in a degloving motion. Viv kneels on the tile before the tub's edge and examines her overgrown cuticle.

'Looks alright to me,' she declares, a valiant attempt to dispel the thickening murk of anxiety. 'But we'll keep an eye on it, okay?'

'Okay.' Beneath her jaw, a single bloody thumbprint.

The next few weeks are bad ones. Approvals on preliminary parts come through late, caught in the net of preferential revisions. Offered substitutions are snubbed. Schedules condensed. Corners cut. She wakes, works, tries to delegate and fails. Viv returns one afternoon from the grocery store to find her crying in the living room, every nail dripping and bitten to the quick. This makes it harder to tell when it starts getting worse.

'Call in,' Viv says from the bathroom floor, dabbing the ruined fingers with iodine. 'Take a mental health day.'

'The couch...'

'Is just a couch. Remember when I spilled that red wine on the rug in the family room? They'll get it out in no time. I'll call tomorrow.' Her eyes, so sweet and honest. 'Take the day.'

She does, and spends all of it checking email. Her nail beds ache when pressed, her side of the sheets dotted with red pinpricks. Viv – concerned, suspicious – makes her sleep in oven mitts until the final revisions are submitted. Her supervisor fast-tracks them, and then everything is okay again.

'See?' Viv says when the pressure begins to lift. 'Now all you need to worry about is healing.'

But she can't – not really. The raw patches close, the white feathers at the edge of each nail fall away. Even the pain goes.

But the bleeding doesn't stop. Encrusted bandages slide off her fingertips by the boxful, wet prints staining her custom mechanical keyboard with each tap. By now, though, she can't bring herself to care. The client's expedited launch is slated for that summer, and she's never missed a launch. Chalk it up to yet another annoying health problem, something to be addressed next time she goes for blood work. Choke down iron and orange juice and keep going.

Viv is busy too: preparing annual reviews and budgets and disciplinary hearings. One of the companies she consults for, she mentions irritably over dinner, is unionizing. 'They've got excellent benefits,' she says, 'eight weeks maternity, health-care perks some people would kill for. I mean, if you really hate it so much, why don't you go work somewhere else?'

One of the parts manufacturers had just unionized, too – a crushing blow to the already painful schedule. She couldn't cut any more time on the engineering's end; it would have to come from manufacturing's allotment in June. The chaos of it all makes her skin prickle, so she breathes carefully and imagines the face of a former therapist – in for four, hold for seven, out for eight. Remember, you are powerless.

God, she can't fucking stand platitudes. Of course she's powerless, and if she was ever in danger of forgetting that fact, the world is already primed to remind her. From childhood, every dismissal, every leer, every mediocre male student or colleague chosen over her was a hammer to the fingers clinging to the world's ladder, and yet here she was. A queer woman eating at the big kids' table, not as a token but as a peer. Undeniable in her value. Brilliant, driven, beautiful. Loved.

Bleeding.

When it moves to her palms, Viv insists they see a doctor. She acquiesces – what is a marriage but a long compromise? – but complains as they sit in the waiting room, her hands mummified in paper towels. 'They'll tell me it's menstrual,' she says, 'or, best case scenario, they run some tests that all come up inconclusive.'

'I'm tired of stripping the sheets. Please don't fight me on this,' Viv says wearily, so she stops.

They wait nearly an hour before the male nurse practitioner, nonplussed, deigns to take her blood: first from her elbow, then from beneath her nails. He requests the date of her last period, and she waits until he looks down at the clipboard to roll her eyes.

'And this is significantly impacting your quality of life?' he asks.

'Yes,' Viv says before she can respond. 'We're extremely concerned.'

'Understandably.' He doesn't sound understanding. 'Have you experienced any unusual stressors in the last few months?'

She almost laughs, glancing at Viv for validation. 'You could say that.' Then, when he doesn't move to record it: 'I'm a senior engineer. One of my projects has been delayed for almost six weeks.'

'Hm. Can I ask where you work?'

Preening, she tells him. This gets his attention. For a moment, his pursed lips twitch, as if testing the flavor of his response.

'Ah,' he says, finally, in a tone so neutral it reads as incredulity. 'I imagine that's a very difficult job.'

'Important, though.'

Beside her, Viv exhales lightly through her nose.

'Of course,' says the nurse practitioner, turning back to his clipboard. 'Not to mention the money.'

He's making fun. If he would meet her gaze, she could verify it off the self-satisfied twinkle in his eyes. When he pricks her disinfected finger to measure blood coagulation, the enjoyment is obvious. Flushed with rage, she leaves a vicious two-star review in the clinic parking lot and spends the rest of the ride home in the backseat with her head between her knees.

The tests come back normal. Of course they come back normal. No change in blood volume, no sharp decrease in platelet count. No sign of hereditary hemophilia. She's anemic and a little low on Vitamin K, but so are most vegetarians. No skin damage, no lacerations but the superficial scabs around her nails.

'These people are idiots,' Viv says once the paperwork has been read and reread. 'Obviously something's wrong. I want a second opinion.'

They get a second opinion, from a real doctor this time. More blood drawn from beneath the bruised skin at the crooks of her elbows while, only a few inches below, it beads thickly, unbidden, from her knuckles.

'Huh,' says the doctor, examining each hand with the focus of an inexperienced palm reader. 'Might be micro-tears in the skin. Let me make some calls.'

The calls take a better part of two hours, long exceeding her lunch break, and she begins refreshing her email with a slick finger. Eight new, cluttering the pristine inbox. The on-site engineer could be hacking through a dozen juniors with a machete and she wouldn't know until she got back to her computer.

'Take the rest of the day,' her wife says.

'I can't.'

'Stop looking at your phone. Look at me. Will you look at me, please?'

In the dismal waiting room – tightly-upholstered chairs, light chipboard desks, low-pile carpet splotched with mysterious stains she'd been counting as a grounding exercise – Viv's eyes were even more startling than usual. A blue so brilliant that men stopped her on the street to offer commentary, as if a beautiful, clear sky was encased beneath the corneas. Each pupil, a perfect launch.

'Is anybody going to die if you don't answer your emails for a few hours?' Viv asks. Then, when she begins to answer: 'No. They aren't.'

'Somebody might. Someday.'

The weather begins to turn. 'Your work is important. I know it's important, and valuable, but I'm worried about you. You can't do all of this yourself. It's too much pressure. And after what happened at the office, and now this...' she pauses. 'They can't expect you to take everything on.'

'They aren't. Oh, baby. Baby, please don't...'

Viv sniffles. 'You shouldn't have to live like this,' she says softly. 'I just want to make sure we're doing everything we can.'

'We are, baby. And I know it looks bad, but I'm really okay.'

And she is. She's not in pain ('on a scale of one to ten...'), and even if she was, she'd never been one to go down easy. Not like her mother, the textbook narcissist. Or her junkie brother, showing up outside her dorm to beg for money with snot smeared on his upper lip. She did the work. She reparented, unlearned, healed and managed all on her own. What's a little blood in the face of all that has happened to her?

Still, Viv insists. She spends long hours on the telephone, shopping around for hematologists, dermatologists, practitioners of every stripe. Appointments are dutifully attended between meetings, on lunches. Weeks pass and the fussing becomes rote – changing sodden bandages to cover new streams flowing over her wrists. The plastic keyboard cover. The countless tests and samples, scrapings, supplements. In the bath, she holds her hands face up to watch pinprick red fountains issue from each individual pore. A film circles the drain. And still no answers.

Work becomes a welcome distraction. Especially the schematics, with their granular adjustments. Find a problem, fix it, repeat. She finds herself chatting more on calls, her hands below the webcam's eye, and stares wistfully over her supervisor's shoulder at the tiny, pixelated view from his office window.

'You know, we'd really love to have you back in-house,' he tells her. 'Security's better. A lot better. I can't promise it's always perfect but–'

'I'm sorry,' she says, 'but for my mental health, I really can't.'

In miniature, he nods. 'Of course. I understand completely.'

He doesn't know about the bleeding thing. Only the other thing, the incident that drove a horde of engineers remote and prompted police tape and armored escorts from the street up to the high-rise entrance. The reason she dreams in crowds and grows nauseated at the reek of other people. The assault on the front steps.

She couldn't believe it when her subordinates – minus one – returned to the office. Weren't they afraid? Hadn't they seen the police photographs, the gash on her cheek? Didn't they know how irrevocably trauma could reduce a woman to a trembling animal, her career destroyed by a single act of pointless violence? The mere thought of the headline – page four, "Demonstrations Ongoing, Junior Engineer Assaulted" – makes her sick. No. Until things are absolutely safe, she is staying where she is.

But then the last of the parts are again delayed, and the client insists on a meeting. There is no one on-site she trusts to discuss the project in detail, her supervisor (bastard! typical!) has jetted off to a "climate summit" in Stockholm with his newest nineteen-year-old, and very important people can only be stymied in conference rooms for so long. Somebody has to go down there. Somebody local.

Viv gives her a Xanax and they drive down together, holding hands in the backseat. Though it hasn't been long, the city looks worse than she remembers: busier, dirtier. The traffic is awful, but the air within the car is cool and quiet. She fiddles with her sweater, plucking at errant threads with the black fingertips of her latex gloves.

'Just tell them you've got eczema or something,' Viv advises while they stare at taillights.

'I'm not going to say anything unless somebody asks.' The possibility seems remote and unimportant, much less immediate than the potential violence at the front doors. She tries not to think about it.

'Well, just in case. It'll just be for a few hours, right? I'll stick around until you're done.' Viv, her voice painfully sweet. 'We can get lunch after.'

'What?' It comes out sharp, distorted.

Viv continues as if she hasn't spoken. 'Maybe at that Mexican place Sammy recommended? Oh, and I've got a coat to pick up too, the wool one. We can–'

'We aren't staying.' Her pulse beats. Her palms feel warm and slick. 'As soon as I'm done, we're going home.'

'Why not? We haven't gone out in...' Viv flicks a glance at the driver, who doesn't look back. 'Besides, with the gloves on it's barely noticeable.'

'This has nothing to do with my hands. I'm not staying in the city, not after what happened. I'm already five minutes from a panic attack as it is.'

'But you've been doing so much better.' Despite her gentle tone, there's a coolness there. A whine. 'It's been almost eight months, and we're already out. Dr C told me that sitting–'

She exhales a shocked laugh. '*Dr C.*'

'Doctor C. Told me. That sitting at home *ruminating* is only making your anxiety worse.' She gestures with one manicured hand. 'For all we know, it's making *this* worse. You cannot keep living in that room, doing your schematics alone in the dark.'

'Where the hell is this coming from? You're supposed to be on my side.'

Viv's gaze shifts, slightly, like the sheen on water as it turns to ice. 'I *am* on your side,' she says. 'I've been on your side for eight years. I've bent over backwards to accommodate all this and you won't step outside your comfort zone for one afternoon with me.'

'Bent over backwards.' The gloves are loosening, saturated. Ready to molt. 'When's the last time you signed your own name on a check, Vivian? When's the last time you checked your bank balance?'

'Enough,' Viv says venomously. 'This has nothing to do with money and you know it. You're acting like a child.'

Her vision goes glossy. 'I'm *sick*.'

To the back of the driver's head, Viv says, 'Not too sick to work. And look.' She indicates the sparse sidewalk, a fully-outfitted police officer already jogging down to the curb to escort her up the stairs to the glass lobby doors. 'There isn't even anyone there.'

But there is. She can hear them, faintly, individual voices chanting around the corner of the building. Even crowded with shapes, the sky is unbearably huge.

'Don't bother staying,' she says, unspooling herself onto the pavement. 'I'll take the subway home, since I'm such a fucking burden.'

'That is not what I–' But the door slams shut before Viv can finish.

Everything goes perfectly. The client, plied with liquor and launch videos, is far more reasonable – and prettier – than anticipated.

'Please, call me Miranda,' she says when referred to by her title, the blue fluorescent light glancing off the understated flag pin on her lapel. 'We're all friends here.'

Miranda's informality does not extend to her entourage, who follow silent as wraiths half a pace behind as they traverse the building. She listens to the explanation of the manufacturer's delay intently, removing a pair of readers from her breast pocket to examine a revised contract. Her hands are lined, her nails scrupulously painted in a flattering, feminine beige. If she notices the gloves when they hand her the clipboard, she makes no mention of them.

'I see,' she says finally. 'I'll have to do some reading, but it's clear my confidence was not misplaced.' Then, 'Are there any pictures of it? I know it isn't finished, but I'd just love to take a look.'

A text is sent to someone on the manufacturing floor four thousand miles away and minutes later, the images are there before them. Unblinking, Miranda exhales through her mouth. Presumably in awe.

'My God. It's incredible. The details... it's so compact. And this was all you?'

'No, no.' She's blushing, tucks a strand of hair behind her ear. 'It's very much a team effort. Dozens of engineers...'

'But you're the watchmaker. You're the artist,' Miranda says. 'I can tell. Don't minimize what you've done. All these...' She waves her hand to conjure the word without speaking. 'They wouldn't hesitate a second to take the credit. Don't let them erase what you've done. What you're doing for all of us.'

In the car home, alone, she's floating. She forgets the spat, bursts through the front door and takes Viv in her arms. They haven't made love in almost two months – too tired, too busy, too *messy* – but tonight they fuck like teenagers. The sheets stiffen in the dark, pulled off the edge of the mattress in bloody fistfuls. When the lights come on, the wallpaper is ruined.

'Why didn't you keep the gloves on?' Viv moans, lying naked on the stained carpet. Her body is streaked in clotted gore like something pulled through the shattered windshield of a car wreck.

'I wanted to touch you.' Running her hands under water does nothing. Rivulets of blood blossom from her undamaged forearms and pool in the sink. 'You're always complaining about how I don't touch you anymore.'

'You can touch me with the gloves on. Ugh, these are my mother's linens... wait, no, don't use that towel! Don't touch anything, I'll get one of the black ones. Don't move, just stand right there.'

Shame makes her face heat, her dry lips buzz. 'You could at least pretend not to be disgusted.'

'I'm not disgusted.' She is. When she stands, liquid beads from beneath her breasts and thighs like raindrops racing on a car window. 'I'm sorry. I'm glad we had sex. This is just a lot and I need you to be patient with me.'

Her flesh is raw from scrubbing. Impossible to tell if the skin is undamaged now. 'You knew I was a lot when you married me.'

Viv is silent, and the silence makes her hackles rise.

'What is it going to take to make you happy?' she snarls. 'Do I work more or not at all? Fuck you or not fuck you? Or are you just waiting for all the sick parts to magically go away? Because I have some very disappointing news.'

Viv, pale and rigid, 'You don't talk to me that way.'

'It's not "in health and health, 'til inconvenience do us part", Vivian. You made a promise to me–'

'*I* made a promise to *you*? *We* made a promise.' She's fighting not to cry now, her brow screwed up. 'I'm not one of your toys. You didn't make me.'

Her vision tunnels. 'You're right,' she says. 'If I made you, at least you'd be useful.' And a moment later: 'Oh, God. God, I didn't mean that. I don't know why I... Baby. Baby, come here. Please come here, I'm sorry. I didn't–'

Liquid splatters the carpet when Viv jerks away. 'There is something really wrong with you,' she says through her teeth. 'Don't come near me.'

'Baby...'

'Don't fucking touch me.' But when the dripping palm finds her shoulder, she doesn't pull away.

They make up, as best they can, but Viv's side of the bed is cold in the morning and stays cold into the small hours. Eventually, she strips the sheets herself. Handprints dry to fecal browns and blacks. To keep from ruining more clothes, she dictates emails to her laptop from the bath and when she does emerge, it's to bind her arms to the elbows with gauze, as if in preparation to box. Working should be impossible, nobody would blame her if she came clean and bowed out, and yet. They're so close.

It's just little things now. Paperwork. Flight permissions. Somebody from comms asking questions about webcast viewer numbers. As the launch looms, activity outside the office increases, with a casualty of three first-floor windows. The evening news shows only a brief clip, followed by extensive coverage of the perpetrator whose arm was broken by security.

Consequences, consequences.

A meager twelve hours before, she flies alone to the desert to watch it happen in person. They treat her like a queen – first class, champagne mixer. At the canapes table, her boss's boss's boss pulls her into conversation. 'Congratulations on your big day. I hear you've been stepping up,' he says into her ear. 'Covering for these fucks.'

This close, she can hear his brain whirring. Conjuring optics, weighing benefit against blowback. 'It's been my pleasure.'

'The client loves you.' He turns his head slightly towards the crush at the bar. Miranda, pink-cheeked, lifts a hand to wave. A moment later, she's beside them.

'Congratulations,' she says. Her eyes are pale blue. How had she failed to notice before? 'I hope I'm not interrupting talk of a promotion.'

The boss laughs, though it's more breath than humor. 'Are you offering a recommendation, ma'am?'

'More than a recommendation.' The corner of Miranda's mouth quirks. 'I can see us working together for a long, long time.' A little laugh. 'Don't you think so?'

Blood is pooling in the fingertips of the latex gloves she's wearing. Soon, it will saturate the second pair on top, then the black opera gloves clasping her glass. 'I'd like that,' she says.

Those eyes. Like polar cores.

'Shall we have a toast, then?' Miranda lifts her glass. 'To the security of our future and our children's.'

'To our children's future.'

'To our children.'

They let her see the satellite before it goes. Down corridors, past dark offices, into the open hangar. In the flesh, it is modest, and sleek, and beautiful. She imagines it breaching the atmosphere, swimming in the stars above. The first of its make, bellowing coordinates and heat signatures back to Earth in streams of cosmic whalesong. It almost hurts to let it go. Her Laika.

'Can I touch it?' she asks. The reflection of her face is crying.

'I'd prefer if you–' one of the techs begins, but she's already working off a glove. A sharp intake of breath behind her. The velvet drips as she presses a thumb to its flank.

'For good luck.' The whorls of the fingerprint have already begun to blur. 'Have fun up there.'

The Authors

Scott Beggs enjoys the taste of virtual beets. His short stories have appeared in *PseudoPod*, *Dark Moon Digest*, *MYTHIC Magazine*, and *All Worlds Wayfarer*. He moves around a lot with his family, and he wants to be Buster Keaton's best friend. Follow him on Twitter @scottmbeggs and visit scottbeggs.com for more.

Phil Cummins is an Irish writer of fiction and non-fiction with work published in *Crannóg*, *Fictive Dream*, *bioStories* and elsewhere. His work has placed in various competitions including The Fish Memoir Prize (Honourable Mention, 2020; Shortlist, 2022), Wild Atlantic Writing Awards (Finalist, 2024), and Fish Short Story Prize (Longlist, 2024).

Corinne Engber is a genre fiction writer and professional working stiff. Her work has appeared in *Lammergeier Magazine*, *Sinister Wisdom* and *Mangoprism*. She lives in Boston with her wife and cat. Find her on Tumblr @synonymsfordismember.

James Everington writes dark, supernatural fiction, although he sometimes takes a break to write dark, non-supernatural fiction. His second collection, *Falling Over*, is out now from Infinity Plus. He's also written *The Quarantined City* ("an unsettling voice all of its own," *The Guardian*) and co-edited the BFS Award-nominated anthology *Imposter Syndrome*.

LL Garland enjoys gaming, writing speculative fiction, and exploring deep, dark woods. She's been called "disturbingly competitive" at all three. She lives in a house with three dogs and two libraries – a fancy one for show, and a hidden one for the weird stuff. You can find more of her stories on her website, **llgarland.com**.

David Hartley writes strange stories about strange things for strange people. His short story collection *Fauna* was longlisted for the Edge Hill Prize. He lives in Manchester and lurks on Instagram **@DHartleyWriter**.

Tim Jeffreys' short fiction has appeared in *Supernatural Tales*, *The Alchemy Press Book of Horrors 2 & 3*, *Nightscript 4*, *Stories We Tell After Midnight 2 & 3*, *Cosmic Horror Monthly #1*, and many other places. His ghost story novella, *Holburn*, was released by Manta Press in 2022. The sequel, *Back from the Black*, came out in 2023. Other work includes the comic horror novella, *Here Comes Mr Herribone!*, and sci-fi novella, *Voids*, co-written with Martin Greaves. Blog: **timjeffreysblogspot.com**

Lauren Mulvihill is a writer and storyteller from Co. Waterford. Her work is inspired by the folklore and legends of Ireland, with a bit of general absurdity sprinkled in. She spends much of her free time writing, thinking about writing, and also knitting.

Lily Nobel is a student of Environmental Studies at Oberlin College. Her recent work be found in *manywor(l)ds*, *Maudlin House*, and *miniskirt magazine*.

Elaine O'Connor is a writer from Dublin. She currently lives in California and is working on her first novel.

Elin Olausson is a fan of the weird and the unsettling, and has published the short story collections *Growth* and *Shadow Paths*. Elin's rural childhood made her love and fear the woods, and she firmly believes that a cat is your best companion in life. She lives in Sweden.

Diana Powell is an award-winning author of short fiction. She is the winner of the 2022 Bristol Short Story Prize. Her novel, *things found on the mountain,* was published by Seren Books last year. Her novella, *The Sisters of Cynvael* (Cinnamon Press), came out in May.

Shalini Srinivasan writes comics, bits of research, and fantasy for children and adults. Her books include *Vanamala and the Cephalopod*, and *Shoecat Thoocat*. She spends a lot of time holding forth at captive students.

Claire Watson is an Irish writer pursuing an MA in Creative Writing at University College Cork. Lover of the queer and the "quare", their short fiction has appeared in *Trans_Muted* and they are a writer for the artbook *Fey: A Guide to Fae of the Butch Variety.*

Rebecca Weinert is a writer, artist, and cat lover who has turned her life-long fascination with stories into a degree in English and Literature that has taught her little about either of those topics. Her stories are either dark and unsettling or pure cosy wish-fulfilment. There is no in-between.

Sans.
PRESS